Holiday Tales Anthology

Celebrating the Important Days of Our Lives

November 2014

Edited by: Lois G. Bennett
Published by: Fireside Publications

Fireside Publications
Oxford, Florida 34484

www.firesidepubs.com

Printed in the United States of America

For additional copies of this book, please visit:
www.firesidepubs.com or
www.Amazon.com

Editor's Comment

Holiday Tales Anthology is offered for reader enjoyment during any of our many holiday seasons of the year. The New Oxford Dictionary, 2nd Ed. defines "holiday season" as the period of time between Thanksgiving and New Year's Day including Christmas, Hanukkah, and Kawanzaa."

The same dictionary defines "holiday" as "a day of festivity or recreation when no work is done. December 25 is an *official* holiday," while the Brits refer to being "on holiday" as a festive time with a holiday atmosphere and entertainment."

When Fireside Publications issued a story callout for submissions for *Holiday Tales,* the decision was made to let the writers decide which holiday tweaked their imagination enough to make them write about it. Thus we have the majority of stories about Christmas – perhaps because we are nearing that season soon – and some about Thanksgiving. Surprisingly, or not, a strong showing was made for Halloween, which was not included in the above definition. Others wrote about Springtime including an Easter fantasy story, and Arbor Day, as well as Independence Day.

One story which struck a special chord with me was initially dubbed a *Christmas* story, but as I read it, I soon realized it was a story of gaining freedom and independence. In her Bio, the author, an immigrant to America, told of her experience after that December when her family first arrived here, and their search for independence. To view America through the experience of a new arrival is truly enlightening, so I chose to include some of her comments along with her story. Another person wrote of an unusual and very special wedding.

Most of the pieces included in this anthology are not the typical sleigh bells or turkey stories one expects in a holiday book. Rather they are an eclectic group of festive occasions viewed by a cross section of writers, who chose to define *holiday* in their own special way. This is how I think it should be. I hope you agree.
Enjoy.

Lois Bennett, PhD

Happy Holidays Everyone

Contents

Contents con'd.

Dedication

This Anthology is dedicated to writers the world over,
who celebrate, record and remember
the special days, of their lives
for future generations to know and continue
the traditions of yesteryear and today
then go on to create their own special brand
of holiday to define a new generation.

Acknowledgements

I am grateful to the many people who gave of their time, effort and advice to see this Anthology through to completion. The authors who, submitted their creative endeavors, some on very short notice, to make it all possible, were the mainstay of the project. Without them, there would be no book.

Joan West, friend and business partner, was responsible for getting me started in this publishing business; she continues to offer advice, critiques, or join me for lunch on short notice when the need arises. Her husband, Glen, patiently waits for the *girl talk* to be over and always reminds me not to lose my *sense of humor.*

Colette Sasina, friend, poet and charming lady can always be counted on for that extra bit of help. She graciously shared several of her poems that so fittingly blended with the stories included in this anthology. Unless otherwise noted, all the poems included herein are from Colette's collection of original poetry.

Jessica Henderson, *My Girl Friday,* will tackle most anything, but like the song says, "I'll do it my way." To her credit, she has rescued this manuscript on several occasions. Her *helpers*, Iulia, Jacob, Kadin and Kira enjoy teasing their *Nana* while she sits with them, so we can work. Nonetheless, I enjoy everybody's help, and we eventually get the job done.

PART ONE

Thanksgiving
&
Celebrations of Life

Turkey Whisperer

Hear ye every tom and hen,
It's turkey time once again.
Your meat is in high demand,
coast to coast across the land.

From wattle to tail -"Bishop's hat,"
your flesh is juicy, plump and fat.
Legs that skitter, wings that flutter-fly-
you must use them now to flee, or die.

If you stick around, try camouflage.
Disguise your feathers with decoupage.
Be a piñata using thick modge-podge.
But the safest of all – Get out of Dodge."

Family at Grandma's house?
Let them all gorge on grouse.

Thanksgiving 1949
by
Colette Sasina

Snow sprinkles gently over Detroit, a winsome white welcome for Santa's arrival at the Thanksgiving Day parade tomorrow. My grandmother, Busha, will visit us for two days; her first and only overnight with us – ever. She will stay in my room and sleep in the bed my papa built *just* for me. I am so excited. I'd rather spend time with my Busha than drive downtown to see the parade with my friend Nancy, who lives across the street, and her Mom.

Busha arrives mid-afternoon with a song in her heart, greeting us with gardenia scented hugs and rosy lipstick kisses. She favors her left leg, always wrapped in an ace bandage below the knee. "Happy Thanksgiving, Margie," she sings, gathering her daughter into her arms. "Happy Thanksgiving, Busha," my Mama returns, then pours a cup of steaming coffee to warm her mother. They waste no time chatting away, rolling dough, making pies, grating cabbage for slaw, toasting bread and browning vegetables for stuffing. Even though I am eight, I sense the sacred bond woven into their non-stop Polish-English banter.

I cover the table with Mama's hand-embroidered tablecloth and set out napkins and silverware. My favorite ritual comes next – retrieve Max, the brown ceramic moose pitcher, from the top shelf of the pantry and give him a soapy wash, quick rinse and dry. Max will share center stage with the woven grapevine cornucopia I fill to overflowing with small lacquered gourds, leaves and dried mums. Max, with his cute curly antlers, inspires funny comments at our holiday dinners.

At bedtime, I climb the stairs to bunk with my brother, Basil. I pause on the landing and feel a wintry draft wafting around my Papa's hand-crafted storm windows. Sparkly frost splatters the panes with lacy snowflakes, lending a fairytale appearance to the brick bungalows lining Yolanda Street below. Smoke billows from furnaces, spiraling to the star-sequined sky. I press my forehead against the cold window and thank Jack Frost for creating his lens to enchantment.

Early Thanksgiving morning, Mama stuffs and brushes the turkey with melted butter. Papa lifts the heavy bird into the roasting pan and slides it into the oven. A dusting of snow overnight records our footprints as we walk two blocks to Church for the 8:00 a.m. Mass. "Good Morning. Happy Thanksgiving," Mama offers to a neighbor who smiles and pulls open the massive wood door. "Happy Thanksgiving to you too." We enter, walk to the front, light a few vigil lights at the side altar, genuflect and find a pew. Bells ring out and Mass begins. We are grateful, warm, content in the moment.

An hour later we arrive home to the savory aroma of roasting turkey. Mama and Busha head straight to the kitchen. I soon hear cranberries popping on the stove, smell sweet potatoes baking in the oven. Basil and I sip eggnog and play a game of Monopoly.

An eternity later, I hear, "It's time to fill Max," an order from the kitchen. Mama mashes potatoes, Busha fills the gravy boat with steaming velvety sauce, Papa ceremoniously platters and places the turkey on the table. He leads us in grace and carves with his usual elegant flair. Thanksgiving dinner is delicious. Every year is better than the last, or so it seems. Mama and Busha share the turkey's tailbone, 'bishop's hat', a holdover from The Great Depression when nothing was wasted. Mama serves coffee. Max, filled with cream, makes his ceremonial pass around the table. I top off my milk, somehow find room for pumpkin pie piled high with whipped cream. "Mincemeat is still my favorite," Papa declares and helps himself to a second piece.

We clear the table, put leftovers in the Frigidaire, wash and dry dishes while Papa takes a short nap. He wakes up with a yawn, grabs his Lionel train engineer's cap and heads to the chilly basement to begin our favorite holiday ritual. First he opens the pot belly stove and damper, fills it with wood and kindling, lights the bundle with a match and closes the small door. He starts up his prized engine and sounds the whistle. Busha joins us all downstairs around the train table. We watch, mesmerized, as the shiny engine pulls assorted railroad cars around the track, click clack; up, down; over the

4

bridge, through his hand-fashioned, landscaped Lilliputian village, whistling and chugging, much like the real McCoy lumbering down the tracks through the crossing a half-mile away. Basil takes over while Papa stokes the fire.

We are warm and cozy; family in communion; real; *Rockwellian.* It was a good year –1949.

First appeared in Yesterday's Magazette

Author Bio: Colette Sasina, poet extraordinaire, is a two-time contributor to Chicken Soup for the Soul. She is a lover of life, nature, and especially her family, and transfers their every attribute to verse. Her poetry is often published in local newspapers, and magazines as well as in online publications. She contributed the poetry found in this anthology, unless otherwise noted. Several of her poems appeared in a non-fiction book on Alzheimer's disease in 2010 by Lois Wilmoth-Bennett, PhD.

Unnoticed Shenanigans?
by
Carol Ray Skipper

"Katie. Enough! You have voiced your complaints. Give it a rest." Mom was not impressed with my *whining*, as she called it, about having to sit at the kids' table for Thanksgiving.

It was Sunday before Thanksgiving. Our annual vacation to Nana and Papa's house had begun. The last count was thirty-two people for the Thanksgiving feast — fifteen relatives, four dogs, and a fat cat were moving in, some for six days. Peace for two old fogies was about to become total chaos.

"Stop!" I yelled, as Dad pulled into the drive way. Just beyond the huge, moss draped oak tree was a flock of young turkeys focused on the hunt for their dinner. My brother and I counted twenty. Oh, yes, don't forget the leader; the hen made twenty-one. They grubbed for acorns, berries, bugs, seeds or small reptiles as they claimed their territorial rights, soon to be invaded by humans.

Last year Papa and I had a conversation about turkeys; so I tried to explain to Kevin, my little brother, who's who in the turkey family.

"The little boys are called 'jakes,' and the little girls are called 'jennys.'"

Kevin thought that was a hoot.

"And the hen, the adult female turkey, is their mommy; and their daddy, the adult male turkey, is called 'tom' or 'gobbler.' He's the one who makes the loud, gobbling noise." Tom was nowhere to be seen, perhaps off strutting his spread of 5,000 feathers.

All of a sudden, twenty-one turkeys froze! They glared at the four yakking humans, two dogs, our fat cat, an extra-large cooler, golf clubs, sleeping bags and suitcases that were stuffed inside, or strapped on top of, Mom's candy-apple red SUV. Noise erupted with their "cackle, cackle, cackle" as they ran.

Casper, our eighty-pound, black Labrador retriever (shaking crate) decided it was time to voice his interest – *twenty-one turkeys! Let me out!* His excited barks brought farts!

"Let Casper out!" I shouted. "He's gross!"

Callie, with a tummy full of kittens due before Thanksgiving, according to her veterinarian, meowed from her crate. Thank goodness, Cuddles, our heavy-weight poodle of four pounds, was oblivious, snuggled inside her tiny, pink, soft-sided travel bag.

"Casper!" Dad snarled.

Casper growled.

Thanks to Casper, our arrival echoed around the world. Nana and Papa raced out to welcome us.

The minute Dad turned off the ignition, seat belts were unbuckled, and my brother and I ran to Nana and Papa. They couldn't believe how much we had grown since last Thanksgiving. My parents managed to sneak in hugs before Casper, Nana and Papa's favorite furry member of the family. He does rate priority; he had his first visit as a puppy, and he just celebrated his twelfth birthday, born on Halloween.

I'm the oldest grandchild, but exactly one-year younger than Casper.

Casper was excited to see Nana and Papa — *I'm back, I missed you. Where are the turkeys?* He took off for a much deserved run.

Please let it help his butt –we had traveled for thirteen hours, North Carolina to Florida.

Cuddles gave her proper hello, took care of business and was ready to go inside. Then Nana and Papa saw Callie. They knew she was expecting kittens, but they had no idea she was HUGE!

"When are the kittens due?" asked Nana.

"Oh, most any minute now," smiled Dad, aka Callie's personal vet.

We were the first of the sleep-over group to arrive. I was thrilled. That meant Kevin and I could sleep in our sleeping bags on the bunk beds, not the floor. I guess that made it worthwhile for getting up so early. Mom and Dad got the guest suite, not one of the pull-out sofas or sleeping bags. Oh man, Aunt Grace is gonna be ticked; no guest suite for her.

"Yes!" Nana's kitchen smelled yummy. She had made her famous chicken and dumplings, her delicious green beans, and corn bread that she fries in an iron skillet. *It is so good.* And she had just taken her lemon-pound cake out of the oven. Sometimes she reminds me that she's old. She may be old, but she sure is a good cook!

Kevin and I were pleased to have Nana and Papa's undivided attention. Morning would soon arrive, and we would have to share them with our idiot cousins. Let's just say some of them I would not have picked to be my relatives. I suppose that happens in most families. As Mom often reminds me, "You can pick your friends, but you're stuck with your relatives."

Too bad.

Actually, there's one who I adore, Julia. She's the daughter of Mom's youngest brother, Uncle Rob. He's a pediatric cardiologist, but he calls Mom for baby advice, makes you wonder what he learned in med school. That's fine, we love it because we get to Skype with Julia. She is cute and funny, she reminds Mom of me when I was a charming two-year old! I can't wait to show Julia the chickens; I can just hear her giggles.

Lucky for her, she gets to sit in her highchair at the adult table. She has mastered the skill of throwing food, so it's just as well that Uncle Rob can have clean-up duty. Trust me, it will not be her mommy, Aunt Grace. Julia's nanny does everything for her in Tallahassee. I have to admit, Aunt Grace is beautiful. And as they say in North Carolina, she "married up." Their barn is bigger than our house, and of course, Aunt Grace drives a fancy BMW. Not too shabby. Aunt Grace better bring her designer sleeping bag.

I'm not allowed to swear, but I'm just saying, if I could, "I would swear that Kevin and I are Nana and Papa's favorite grandchildren." Kevin can be a brat, that's his job; he's a six-year-old boy. And for me, I am known to whine if things don't go my way, you know, just being a preteen girl. I guess we're typical kids. But you better believe we show our best behavior to Nana and Papa. Trust me, it works. We go home with extra-special gifts, that not even Mom and Dad know about until we are back in North Carolina. Nana and Papa are proud grandparents, Papa is known to brag. He tells his friends that I study French and I'm in the gifted program. He's a retired attorney, and his favorite daughter, my mom, is an attorney also. They're adamant that I will be an awesome attorney, something about my skill to debate until I win. Attorney is good, but I believe "Your Honor" gets the final word. I'll have to work on that.

Kevin played a game on his iPad.

I read.

Casper snored.

I could hear Dad talking to Callie. I climbed off the top bunk and ran to find Callie and Dad. They were in Mom and Dad's bathroom. "Is it time?"

"Shhh," Dad whispered. "Callie needs to be calm, and yes, I believe we will have kittens by morning. It was 11:00 p.m.; I questioned his estimated time of delivery.

"Well, Miss Katie, morning could be anytime after midnight."

Dad had fixed Callie a bed in a cardboard box; she kept digging at the bed and rearranging the old, soft towel. Things could get a little messy so Dad wanted to be able to dispose of the birthing bed and give her a clean bed when she was ready to move her kittens. Mom and Dad suggested that I go back to bed.

"Please let me stay. I'll be quiet. I want to be with her. Plus Dad, you talk about it all the time, how natural it is for animals to give birth. I wanta watch."

"What's happening? Why are you guys in the bathroom?"

"Kevin, you need to go back to bed. Dad's taking care of Callie." Mom explained as she hurried Kevin back to the bunk room. Mom returned with my pillow and sleeping bag. Casper and Cuddles joined me on the floor, with a perfect view of Callie, just outside the bathroom door.

Dad moved a lamp to the bathroom to make it cozy; Callie seemed calmer. Dad rubbed Callie's head and talked softly to her. Mom made hot chocolate, probably thinking I would join her. No way. I wasn't going anywhere.

Callie gave a big meow.

"Oops! Gross! What's that?" My eyes were big as watermelons.

"That, my Dear, is a kitten. Congratulations Callie, you're a mommy! And you just had a perfect delivery." It was 12:05 a.m.

"You call that perfect! I call it gross! I'm glad Kevin left. Will they all look like that?"

"She'll clean them up and then they'll be all soft and cuddly."

My dad's the best. I took a break from the birthing room and drank my hot chocolate in the kitchen with Mom. *When we returned, Callie was licking her second kitten. "Two out an*d two to go," said Dad.

I reached in the box to rub Callie.

"You're a good mommy".

Out slid another kitten. Callie stayed busy, as she licked all the nasty mess off the kittens. Then came another one. Poor Callie; she was exhausted.

Yes, it was messy, and now, at the mature age of eleven, I have done that and don't care to ever do it again. Hate to tell Dad, but after that experience, I'm pretty sure I will not be a vet.

I awoke the next morning and saw four of my cousins, asleep in the bunk room – girls in the bottom beds, boys on the floor.

Casper and Kevin had vanished.

I peeped out the window and saw the flock of little turkeys and their mommy. I ran to check on Callie and her kittens. I knocked on the bathroom door, but no answer. I eased open the door; there was the proud mommy with her sleeping babies. Dad had given instructions not to touch the kittens, yet. Callie needed a little time to bond. I let them be.

Everybody was in the kitchen: Nana, Papa, Mom, Dad, Kevin, Casper and Cuddles. The relatives who had arrived around 3 a.m. were still asleep. Mom's oldest brother and his family, and their slobbery bulldog, had driven from Atlanta. The "Wild Kid" family: boys, ages six and five, and twin girls, age four. They're like from another planet, and they destroy everything.

Cuddles runs under the bed; she will have nothing to do with them. Even Cuddles recognizes destroyers!

We have to have changing of the guard for Callie and her kittens. I'm confident Dad or Casper can handle the wild and crazy cousins and their dog, Murphy.

Mom, Kevin and I took off for a day at the beach, while Nana and Papa visited with the Atlanta relatives. Mom was pleased that she would not have to referee Kevin and the cousins. Being a little precocious, I have learned to avoid the Atlanta cousins, unless they are under the supervision of sane adults, not their parents. As Kevin matures, he'll learn how to outsmart them, too.

Days were going quickly, it was now Wednesday and our Orlando relatives, Mom's middle brother and his wife, would arrive before dinner. Hopefully, no more cracked eggs and the kids' toilet would be unclogged, and stay useable. It appears the warriors had been busy; and because of this, they had spent a lot of time restricted to the porch. Papa threatened to tie-up their legs. Some adults had gotten a little testy.

I went grocery shopping with Nana and Papa for last-minute items. "Have you ever had fish for Thanksgiving?" I asked.

You should have seen their faces as they rolled their eyes at each other, with their mouths wide-open.

"We always have turkey!" said Nana, "with my special mashed potatoes and gravy, my delicious stuffing, fresh green beans, cranberry sauce, corn bread and pumpkin pie. And sometimes I add my sweet potato casserole. Katie, why on earth would we have fish?"

"Nana, it's fine. I was just curious."

"What kind of fish do you like?" asked Papa.

"Grilled Salmon, it's my favorite."

"I agree, that's a delicious fish."

I went to the restroom while Nana and Papa paid for the groceries and then met them at the check-out counter. Not another word about fish.

It was Thanksgiving eve, and all the kids were clean. The adults, except Nana, had gone out to a movie. Nana popped lots of popcorn. Kevin and the cousins watched a video, and I challenged Nana to a game of scrabble. Nana and Papa's family room was calm; Nana was in complete control of six kids, three dogs, a mama cat and four kittens. No biting or fighting, no spilled juice, and no frog in the bunk room. All the pee was aimed in the toilet and the bathroom floor was dry.

There's maybe no need for any shenanigans tonight.

Nana and Papa could teach a class on *How to celebrate Thanksgiving.* They never cease to amaze me. The number for Thanksgiving had increased to thirty-nine. Thank goodness Papa will say his special blessing over the food, the cooks and the many people who have gathered to celebrate Thanksgiving. If everybody spoke, it would take days. Nana and Papa's friends know something about everything, and the relatives never shut up. My grandparents should have a swinging door. They welcome everyone to their home and they call each one a 'close friend'. I suspect they have 3,000 close friends!

Nana and Papa are believers of delegation. Everybody has a job, and Nana is the boss. My uncles set up the extra tables and chairs, take the little boys for a run on the property, water Nana's flowers and if need be, go play putt, putt (act like a Florida tourist); in other words, stay out of the house! Papa and Dad cook the turkeys, outside. My newest aunt, from Orlando, will fold the silverware into the napkins. The twins and their mom will organize (cleanup) the toys, the foyer and the kids' bathroom.

Anything Nana needs, Mom will do. By being the oldest grandchild, Nana has declared me the official *food taster*, that is, if Papa is not nearby. Nana, aware that Julia will arrive momentarily, will keep me available to introduce Julia to lots of new things: chickens, kittens, cousins. OMG, she'll be so excited.

Casper will guard Callie and her kittens. Cuddles will hide, and Murphy has yard duty – he will bark when people arrive.

Thanksgiving had started to come together. Murphy continued to bark. The additional dishes of food looked awesome. The kitchen smelled delightful. In spite of my complaints, I had not negotiated a seat at the adults' table. I don't know how long I will tolerate the table manners of the other kids. Oh, well, one of Nana and Papa's rules, the oldest at the table gets first serving. Thank goodness that's me.

I heard giggles. I knew it was Julia. I charged out of the kitchen and ran to find her and Aunt Grace and Uncle Rob. I squatted to hug her as she ran into my open arms.

"Katy! Katy! Katy!" she squealed.

I couldn't believe how much she had changed since last Thanksgiving, a drastic difference in a one-year-old and a two-year old. In spite of seeing her on an almost daily basis via the internet, I was swept away with how incredible it was to hear her jabber and see her run. And, she was so much bigger. A quick hug for Aunt Grace and Uncle Rob, but I didn't see Roxie, their yellow Lab. I scooped up Julia and ran outside before Mom or Nana could claim rights to hug and kiss her. Julia and I had lots of things to do and so little time. She tried to say everything I said, and she slaughtered the word *squirrel*. I yelled for Uncle Rob to bring his iPhone so he could video Julia.

"Where's Roxie?" I asked.

"Our vet offered to keep her, and since her puppies are due in two weeks, we took his advice and decided not to have Roxie endure an extended road trip. Trust me, Roxie is fat and happy," Uncle Rob smiled.

I nodded. *Good decision, one less dog to keep away from the kittens.*

Julia was thrilled to meet the chickens – can't report that the chickens reciprocated. Julia jabbered the whole time we were with them. I don't know who had the best time; actually, I do, Uncle Rob. He loved to see his little girl so excited. Now that she could talk, (jabber, jabber) and run, she was full of herself on a new adventure at Nana and

Papa's country home. She wanted no part of going back inside, but I had to share her with the other relatives, especially Nana.

Julia, coaxed by Uncle Rob, gave Nana a quick hug. Julia will learn that Nana is a relative you want on your team. But on this day, at the prime age of two, she declared me her favorite.

Thank you, Julia.

"Get ready to take another video." I carried Julia. Today Uncle Rob was just being Julia's Dad, not a world-known doctor who helps really, really sick children.

"Shhh," I whispered as we entered Callie's nursery. I assured Callie that we would be careful. I held Julia in my lap, Callie and Casper on guard as I lifted one of the kittens. Julia and I held the soft, yellow kitten.

The tiny kitten smelled so clean.

Julia was mesmerized. Her jabber-jabber stopped.

Uncle Rob was amazed at Julia's quietness and how gentle she was with the tiny kitten. For sure, a video that will be shared hundreds of times. I whispered to Julia, "It's time for the kitten to take a nap."

"Nite, nite," Julia whispered.

Uncle Rob had put their stuff in Mom and Dad's room; Aunt Grace was clueless that her bed was the family room floor. We did a quick diaper change, six hands washed and off to the kitchen.

Nana and Papa invited their family and friends to gather together; I squeezed between Dad and Papa. Each person reached for a hand to hold. I held hands with two of the kindest, nicest, smartest people I knew.

The faucet dripped.

Papa said the blessing, and then he uncovered three huge turkeys and a steaming grilled salmon.

"Ah! Papa! You did it! Thank you. I love you, Papa."

Papa smiled.

I gave him a big hug.

A new tradition.

I served myself. The other kids got help from their parents. After piling my plate with mashed potatoes, I surveyed the immediate area and gave the giant spoon a lick.

"Gross! Who licked the spoon?" I yelled. *No one owned up to the crime, imagine that.* I went to the meat area; Mom served me salmon; Kevin chose turkey.

Finally, all the kids were captured by the yummy food.

"Stop it!" I shouted. "Who did it? Who kicked me?" They all stared at each other and shook their heads.

"Who farted?" I screamed.

"Katie, sounds like you're being attacked. Come sit by me," said Papa.

I smiled as I took a seat at the adults' table, next to Papa, on the piano bench.

"Bon appetit," I whispered.

Yes!

Author Bio:

Carol Ray Skipper migrated from Goldsborough, N. Carolina to a small farm in N. Central Florida. Semi-retired, Carol enjoys family time, reading, writing, traveling and spoiling her Labradoodles. Her first published book, appropriately titled, *Coco, the Homeless Labradoodle,* has a sequel "in the making." She recently completed a children's picture book, illustrated by pediatric patients at UF Health Shands, pending release in Spring 2015 with all proceeds going to the Arts in Medicine Program at Shands. Her poetry has been published in Senior Times and in Bacopa, a Literary Review. Carol holds membership in Florida Writers Association, Society of Book Writers and Illustrators, and Writer's Alliance of Gainesville.

The Celebration Quilt
by
Colette Sasina

Son Michael and his wife Dianna treated me to lunch on a cool St. Louis autumn day. After we ordered, Michael sipped his water and said, "Di and I have a vision, Mom – a T-shirt quilt to celebrate our histories.

"What a creative idea," I offered. "The shirts could be icons for your memoirs someday."

Steaming bowls of French Onion Soup soon arrived. Di passed around the baguettes, smiled and added, "We'd love it if you would construct our quilt for us."

I swallowed hard, my mind racing. Crocheting a half dozen granny square quilts did not qualify me for this complex project. Their exuberant mood proved empowering. When chocolate mousse arrived, I decided to give it a try – the quilt that is.

Before I could change my mind, we drove to the fabric store across the street. Di selected what seemed like miles of sky-blue denim, a bolt (the whole nine yards) of cotton backing, navy denim to outline the squares, notions and puffs of quilting fluff – whatever that was. No pattern. *Yikes! What did I agree to?*

"How big is the quilt going to be?" I asked, totally unnerved.

"Queen Size," Di responded.

"Mother of God, please help me."

My faithful 35-year-old sewing machine, Bessie, groaned as Michael and Di crammed three ginormous bags of materials against her cabinet in the laundry room. Then he brought in 42 shirts and quickly reduced each one to a square, using his hand-fashioned cardboard template and my *Edward Scissorhands* extra-long shears which were perfect for the job. He made another template for me to cut out the many mullions to frame each shirt.

They arranged and rearranged their vintage squares on the living room carpet: adventures, sports, social events, alma maters, and one for Missouri Boys State. I noticed a modern art portrait of Di painted by her best friend, a winter frat dance she attended, and several others I would learn about later. I took a picture of the fabric mosaic.

"Thank you so much Mom," I heard in stereo as they left for the five hour drive to Chicago.

My eyes misted glancing at Michael's contribution, familiar shirts I washed and folded through the years. *Edina Cub Softball* when he was seven – "Sorry Mr. Rudin. We'll fix your front window right away." I smiled remembering the incident then picked up his yellow *Rubik's Cube Champion* shirt he won in Jr. High, earning the respect of his peers. I eyed his winning design on the French Club shirt from Parkway Central High School, along with his Colts basketball team jersey. He designed the *Sasina Marina Complete Pool Service* shirt he proudly wore working summers with his Dad and siblings to save money for college. I picked up the shirts one row at a time and stacked them on the dining room table.

Visions of bobbins 'n bolts of material danced in my head as I tossed and turned all night. Fortified by two cups of coffee I began constructing the quilt early the next morning, trying to sew at least two hours, five days a week.

My husband John cleaned and oiled overworked Bessie every 20 hours. It took forever to finish the first row and several more months to sew up the rest. Assembling the strips became more challenging as the quilt grew larger. The final assembly, front to back with fluffy stuff in the middle befuddled me, and almost broke my lightweight Bessie's back. I visualized this massive quilt billowing in the sea breezes, as a mainsail moving a tall ship, as a colorful umbrella being pulled up by the wind, lifting me high in the air to parasail over God's green earth.

In actuality, I was tethered by the sheer weight of the project, mentally and physically. I resolved to take it to completion, and I did – nine months from the first stitch to the last. I named the quilt *Jumanji* after the newly released chaotic film of the same name. Like my complex quilt, it validated the underlying order in chaos.

I proudly presented my creation to the appreciative couple after a celebratory dinner. Michael raised his glass in *joie de vivre* and announced that he and Dianna's very own nine-month creation was underway. They would name her *Amanda*.

Author Bio:
Poet, Colette Sassina, after fervently trying to convince her *"Writer's Bloc"* friends, that she could never write prose, submitted this story to Chicken Soup for the Soul where it made it to the final cut. An avid traveler, Colette pens her poetry while John drives, as they crisscross the country to visit their children. *The Celebration Quilt* first appeared in Yesterday's Magazette.

My Auntie's Wedding

A Short Story

by

Stephen L. Kanne

At 5'8" my Auntie May-Ling is tall, at least by Chinese standards. She is also regal and strikingly handsome. When I attended her wedding at Hong Kong's Peninsula Hotel two weeks ago she was seventy-one years of age but had the figure of someone thirty years younger, a figure set off at the time by the off-white silk Versace gown given to her by her future husband on which she had pinned two pieces from her magnificent jade jewelry collection. As always, her hair was cut short and brushed back, a habit she had acquired during her four years at far off Wellesley College from which she graduated in 1950. When she exchanged her vows of marriage that night, I knew I had fulfilled a promise made many years before: I had brought happiness to my Auntie.

Young people are impressionable, and I was no exception. When I was eighteen something occurred which I shall always remember. My Auntie and I were alone in her Hong Kong apartment enjoying what you in the West call floral tea – tea from pods resembling snail shells which, when immersed in boiling water, burst into flowers. We were seated in her living room watching a lotus blossom unfold as if captured by time-lapse photography. The beauty of the moment gave me the courage, so I asked her a question long hidden in my secret thoughts: *why had someone so kind and so beautiful as she never married?*

My Auntie didn't answer; instead, she began to weep quietly. Ashamed and embarrassed, she excused herself and retired to her bedroom.

When she returned a short time later I swore never to ask her this again. Satisfying my curiosity was a selfish endeavor. But still, I wanted to know. I suspected that my Auntie was the victim of unrequited love – and oh how wrong my suspicions would later prove to be!

Out of respect for her, I changed the subject. I told her of my recent acceptance by Stanford University, of my determination to

17

perfect my English, and of my desire to become a great surgeon. We spoke of all this until the sun disappeared. Walking back to my family's apartment afterwards, I vowed – perhaps childishly – that someday I would arrange a marriage for my Auntie. I thought this would bring her happiness.

And now, looking back upon the grand event of just two weeks ago, I know I succeeded. But it turned out that arranging my Auntie's nuptials, was the most challenging and difficult task of my life – far more difficult than mastering English or perfecting my surgical skills. That her wedding occurred at all is nothing less than a miracle, one which must have been helped along by divine intervention.

Each and every year, as the holiday season approaches, I give thanks to have been a part of this miracle in another person's life.

What I am now about to relate to you came from another; and thank the good Lord that it did, for who would want to bear witness to such horrors?

In March of my senior year at Stanford I was beginning my final term – at the same time looking forward with anticipation to entering its medical school in the fall. One of my courses, *Twentieth Century World History,* was taught by Professor William Bethany Farr, someone we students all revered. In the third week of the term, he began to discuss man's inhumanity to man. He spared no detail. He started by describing the atrocities perpetrated by the Nazi's on Jews, gypsies, homosexuals, and political dissidents. And then he proceeded to tell us of the rape of Nanking by the Japanese military, something I had never known about: *in December, 1937, and January 1938, they had slaughtered thousands of my fellow Chinese.*

Nanking! The city of my late mother's birth; where she and my auntie had been raised. Why had I never heard of this? Perhaps Professor Farr was mistaken. Yes, he must be talking about some other place – not Nanking!

As if anticipating my skepticism, the following day Professor Farr brought a scrapbook to class. And there they were – photographs so horrible I could hardly bring myself to look at them; pile upon pile of corpses; severed heads, pummeled bodies; stacks of limbs and body parts. And then I saw something which changed my life forever: *the photograph of a young girl in her teens, lying on the ground naked in a pool of blood, impaled by a long ugly bamboo shaft rising from in between her legs.* I recognized her immediately – *my Auntie!* A sickening feeling took hold of me as I rushed from the room. In the hallway I began to convulse before finally collapsing to the floor.

There has rarely been a day since first viewing that photograph that I have not thought of my Auntie. Oftentimes during medical school my mind would stray, and I would see her lying there. The pain she must have been in! The scaring to her body that mutilation must have caused! I was beginning to understand why it was that she had never married. I could only imagine the shame she must have felt knowing that she had been rendered less than half a woman.

During the summer following graduation from medical school, I must confess that I thought little of my Auntie. I was selfishly focused on being accepted into a surgical residency program, something normally unavailable to a woman. But, as luck and hard work would have it, I succeeded. And, thus, almost four and one-half years after first viewing that photograph, here I was, seated alone in a corner office of the Weinberg Building at Johns Hopkins University School of Medicine in Baltimore, awaiting the arrival of the Chief of its Surgical Residency Program, Dr. Phillip Galanter. While moving into my apartment earlier in the week I had received a call from the Medical School asking me to make an appointment to meet with him as soon as convenient.

As I glanced around the office, I saw that it was unusually austere. On the desk there was only a framed photograph of an elderly couple – undoubtedly the good doctor's parents. Odd – no photos of his wife and children. And on the wall hung a single diploma: *Harvard College, 1948.* But nothing else – not a pen, pencil, blotter or calendar. Not even a piece of paper. Just then the door behind me opened, and a tall, handsome gray-haired man wearing a white coat entered. I immediately got to my feet.

"None of that, Dr. Bonnie Lu. If we're going to work together, I can't have you jumping up every time I enter the room."

"Sorry, sir," I said

"I don't have much time, so let's begin."

He smiled.

"Any idea why you are here? We don't take many women, you know." He waited for me to reply, but I really had no idea how to answer.

"Here, take a look at this."

He handed me a letter.

"Seems Stan Boetcher thinks you're kind of a wonderkid."

Dr. Boetcher had been my anatomy professor in medical school, and I saw that he had written the letter. I began to read:

Not only did she finish at the top of the class, but I haven't seen hands like hers in years. I can't imagine a finer surgical resident."

As I read on, I blushed.

"Well, Dr. Lu, you ready to go to work?"

I nodded.

Thus began my surgical residency at Johns Hopkins. That first day I was taken to an anatomical laboratory where, under the tutelage of a staff surgeon, I removed the parotid gland from three cadavers. While I was working on the forth, Dr. Galanter entered the lab.

"So, how we doing?" he asked, as he walked from gurney to gurney examining my handiwork.

"What I thought," Dr. Galanter said, almost as If talking to himself. Then, turning to me, he continued. "You up to meeting me in OR #12 at 6:00 a.m. tomorrow morning for the real thing, Dr. Lu – a parotidectomy? You'll be doing the operating. I'll only be assisting."

Although slightly afraid, I managed to say that I'd meet him there. I sensed that this was my first real test. And I knew that dissecting any organ from a living person was far easier than dissecting it from the leathery tissue of a cadaver.

The surgery went well. Dr. Galanter opened and closed, and I removed the gland. Later I was to learn that the patient was a famous celebrity whose career would have ended had I severed or nicked her facial nerve. And, fortunately, her tumor was benign.

In the ensuing months I came to realize that Dr. Galanter was my mentor, and that I would be working closely with him throughout my residency. We lunched often, and it was not uncommon for us to be together in the OR two or even three mornings a week. As is typical in such cases, a special bond quickly developed between us. But I still knew nothing of his personal life.

On the third day of November in my second year of residency, I turned twenty-eight. To my delight, Dr. Galanter and a group of my fellow residents threw a surprise birthday party for me at a local restaurant. I felt both honored and happy.

At last, I thought, *I will learn something of Dr. Galanter's private life – perhaps even meet his family.*

But Dr. Galanter arrived alone. Later that evening after he'd consumed more than a few glasses of wine, I felt his fatherly arm around my shoulder:

"Time for me to go, birthday girl," he said.

Then he hesitated.

"You know, in all these months I've never seen you out with anyone. Take it from one who knows, Bon: *that makes for a lonely life.*" His voice trailed off as he headed for the cloak room.

The following spring Dr. Galanter introduced me to Patrick Wiley, one of Hopkins top urologists.

"You and Pat are going to be working together on a project he and I have a special interest in. He'll tell you all about it, Bon."

From the tone of his voice, I realized that I was entering a new phase of my residency – and, from what I could gather, a fairly important one.

"So here's the skinny," Dr. Wiley began. "We've got two choices with carcinoma of the prostate: either we castrate them or we take out their prostates. Castration doesn't really work – at best it only slows down the disease, so I don't much like it. Taking out the prostate can be a cure, but it has its drawbacks – incontinence and impotence. Only about six percent of our patients become incontinent, but one hundred percent wind up impotent – and that's what you and I are gonna change.

"How?" I asked.

"The nerve bundles – we're gonna take that little puppy out and leave those nerve bundles intact. It's a tricky dissective surgery, but I know we can do it. At least from what I hear I know for sure you can."

"So if the nerve bundles are left behind, there should be no erectile dysfunction?"

"Correct, Dr. Lu," he replied, smiling. "Our patients are gonna be whole men when they leave here, *not half-men.*"

Not half-men!

It was as if an alarm had sounded – *my Auntie, less than half a woman, and Dr. Galanter's special interest in this project.* I decided to risk everything. "And how long ago did Dr. Galanter have his prostate out?" I asked.

Dr. Wiley looked at me in surprise.

"Years ago. But how in the hell do you know about that?"

"We're very close, sir. I guess you'd say there isn't much I don't know about him. We just don't talk about these kinds of things openly."

I looked up. To my relief, Dr. Wiley appeared to accept my somewhat evasive answer.

So there you have it – two extraordinary special people, each with a secret impediment to happiness. Could I bring them together? I would try.

Over the next few weeks I began to tell Dr. Galanter about my Auntie, a beautiful charming woman, a Wellesley College graduate two years his junior, who, as a young girl had suffered a brutal disfigurement of her private parts – and how this shamed her into a life of loneliness. He seemed to understand, even to relate to what had happened to her. I told him she would soon be coming to stay with me.

And then I telephoned my Auntie in Hong Kong.

"I need you here." I said. "I will send you a plane ticket."

When she arrived, I told her of my mentor at Hopkins who had been rendered impotent by a surgeon's scalpel and had chosen to forego marriage and family. "You must meet him." I said.

At first, she refused. But after my persistent urging over a period of many weeks, she eventually agreed.

Thus it was that Dr. Galanter and my Auntie came to know one another. Soon I recognized a friendship beginning to blossom between the two – a closeness which neither had previously experienced. Several months later I saw them holding hands as they walked through the hospital. It therefore came as no surprise when, not long after that, my Auntie told me she and Dr. Galanter were to be married.

My Auntie, Dr. Galanter and I were seated on a large sofa in an anteroom adjacent to the Peninsula Hotel's grand ballroom where the wedding ceremony was to take place in less than one hour. My Auntie saw me look at my watch.

"There's more than enough time," she said.

On the coffee table directly in front of us a large clear spherical glass bowl filled with boiling water rested atop a sterling silver warmer. Flames from the warmer's candles lapped at the bowl's sides.

I saw my Auntie reach into a silken sac and withdraw two small gray objects. She dropped them into the bowl. I wanted you here to see our love unfold," she said, smiling first at me and then at her future husband.

22

As if on cue, two magnificent flowers burst into bloom. Curling upwards, they appeared to embrace one another. "We won't have the luxury of taking our love for granted, Bonnie. We know that. And we'll have to count our blessings each day."

Then my Auntie took hold of Dr. Galanter's hand and gently pressed it to her cheek.

So how do I feel knowing that my Auntie is married and that I've finally brought happiness to her? Exactly as my wise and learned preschool teacher, Mrs. Wong, said I would: *sated with contentment.*

"Learn this proverb well, child," I remember her telling me, so many years ago:

Contentment comes to the maker of a promise kept.

"So keep every promise you make."

"I will," I recall replying.

And, thankfully, with the help of good fortune, and sometimes even divine intervention, so far I have.

Author Bio:
Harvard grad, Stephen L Kanne served in the Army as a reporter/editor. He later attended Stanford Law School, and practiced R. E. Law for over three decades. His short story, *My Auntie's Wedding,* won the 2006 Stanford fiction Contest. In 2010, Steve's first novel, The Furax Connection, a military *boot-camp mystery* from the Korean War era, was published by Fireside Publications and is available on their website: www.firesidepubs.com and on Kindle. Steve and wife Claudia, a documentary film creator, live in Colorado during the summer months, and spend winters in Los Angeles.

SNOW

Ice skates, skis, shiny snowboards,
firewood stacked by the cord,
runners waxed so sleds can go
fast when it finally snows.
A carrot nose, formal top hat,
snowman will look dapper in that.

Soon the north wind blows.
Clouds burst forth with snow.

White forts piled high with spheres,
propelled at those who venture near.
From the gondola or the lift,
high above the wind-carved drifts,
are panoramic views, crystal clear,
a frolicking fawn and red-nose deer.

The mountain boasts champagne powder.
Racing snowmobiles are much louder
than horse drawn sleighs, bells a ringing.
Families are joyously singing.
Blankets cover them as they go,
sipping hot chocolate/marshmallow.

The Sunshine State is too mild for snow.
My retired shovel sports a big, red bow.

PART TWO

The Christmas Holidays
Celebrating a Power Higher Than Ourselves

The Awakening

For a moment, let us take pause
set aside the plans of Santa Claus.

Turn out the lights, burn a candle
listen to the halleluia's of handel.

Picture a manger where lay our Messiah
hear Mary's utter contentment via
soulful lullabies she sings to her baby
as Joseph looks on, a little shaky.

Look east to the heavens for the brightest star
know that the three kings will travel from afar
to present gold, frankincense and myrrh
as shepherds adore, wherever they are.

The magi bring wishes for good will and peace
to our Savior swaddled in new woven fleece
that He may live long as God's Son
till in saving us, His earthly work is done.

Awaken and live the Christmas meaning
enjoy serenity, faith and love's gleaning . . .

Amor Fati
An Orphan's Love Of Christmas!
By
Denise Kingsley

While playing in our front yard, my mother called me to say goodbye to my father. Because of his dreaded disease, tuberculosis, I was trained to stay away from him. I ignored my mother's request.

She made another attempt to get my attention by removing a silk flower from her hat and offered it to me as a bribe; I took the flower and continued to ignore her request. Moments later, I watched two men carry my father from the house to the car. The disease was in his bones and he couldn't walk. Like an unemotional observer, I turned my head to follow the black car slowly take him away.

My father died in the hospital three days after leaving our house; he was only twenty-nine years old.

Our relatives expressed fear that we could bring the disease to their family. No one would chance taking us into their home. My mother had no choice but to place us in an orphanage until she could figure out what to do.

That is why my three brothers and I went to live at Hotel-Dieu, an orphanage in Quebec, Canada. I was five years old.

I would live at Hotel-Dieu for the next five years. The Grey nuns, a Canadian order of Roman Catholic Sisters, ran the orphanage and spoke only French. I, too, spoke only French.

Once I became familiar with the daily routine, I began to feel a sense of belonging and permanence. I had found my tribe. The orphans were my friends, and the Sisters were my surrogate mothers, teachers, nurses, cooks and cleaning crew.

At a young age, I learned to listen and trust the voice of my intuition. Through my feelings, I concluded that my world at the orphanage was a safe and special place.

Without a doubt, Christmas at Hotel-Dieu was my favorite holiday; it was a season of wonder and excitement.

Every floor was decorated, the Sisters were giddy, and there was a détente throughout. On the morning of December 8th, we woke up to the smell of fresh pine, and were greeted by the sight of a beautifully decorated Christmas tree. Baby Jesus was absent from the manger until Christmas Eve; that is when the orphans were paraded on the different floors of Hotel-Dieu.

Except for the orphans, most of the residents at Hotel-Dieu were old and needed constant help. We received lots of hugs and candies when we visited the aged residents. I felt uncomfortable when old people hugged me; they smelled different and wanted us to stay with them. One old man drooled all over my hair. I wanted to run out of his room, instead, not to get in trouble, I slowly joined my group already lined up in the corridor.

There were attempts by the kind Sisters to keep my brothers and I connected, especially during the holidays. On Christmas Eve, my ninth birthday, Sister walked me to the parlor for a surprise visit with my three brothers. I learned that my middle name was "Noella," because I was born on Christmas Eve.

During our visit, my brothers and I stared at each other for what seemed an eternity. We hardly saw each other; we lived on different floors, and had little to say. I was anxious to return to my floor and join my "clan."

The yearly holiday bazaar offered me one of the rare occasions to act as a big sister to my younger brother Marc. The bazaar was a festive day held in a bright hall full of toys, candies and Christmas music. The smell of popcorn and beignets made my mouth water in anticipation of tasting the colorful treats. Each orphan received 40 cents to spend at the bazaar. Marc and I merged our monies, 80 cents was a small fortune. With ten cents I bought him a tiny, black porcelain doll sleeping in a red straw basket. He always liked playing with dolls; inevitably the older boys teased him and broke his dolls. When passing by the boys' playground, through the chain linked fence, I was able to console him and replace his broken dolls.

I do not remember what I did with the rest of our money; it may have been one of the nights I spent at the infirmary because of a stomach ache from eating too much candy. At the infirmary, Sister gave you a glass of red wine to drink in one gulp; you slept soundly till morning.

Another favorite holiday tradition was the visit from the *Chevaliers de Colomb*, known in the US as the Knights of Columbus.

They came bearing gifts and swings for the playground. To prepare for their visit, we practiced singing and dancing for weeks, it was our way of saying *thank you*. Following our performance, each visitor picked an orphan to spend the day together. I turned on my joyous smile, and more than one visitor chose to spend the day with me, which meant more gifts. After our visitors left, Sister allowed me to keep a favorite toy. I usually kept a doll, and I shared the other gifts with girls who had less. I learned non-attachment early, and I was comfortable sharing.

My joyous smile proved to be one of my greatest gifts, especially during the holiday. It gave me the opportunity to get out of the orphanage and accompany Sister to beg for money and enter the homes of local villagers. Most of the parishioners were devoted Catholics of French descent, and they believed that it was an honor, and maybe a shortcut to heaven, for a family to invite a Sister and an orphan into their home for lunch. The fact that I was a skinny orphan probably added to the family's desire to feed me.

Before ringing the doorbell, Sister would remind me of my table manners.

"Don't speak unless spoken to; and smile."

Lunch was a feast for my eyes, but almost as delicious was the warm feeling of spending time with a family who welcomed me with grand fanfare, put out their best dishes, served a special meal and complimented Sister on a charming orphan to accompany her.

For months we practiced singing French Christmas Carols for the Midnight Mass. During Mass, Sister sang soprano, and I accompanied her by singing alto. The parishioners turned their heads to look back at us; some had tears, but they seemed happy to hear us sing. I looked for my mother in the crowd, but to my chagrin, she was not there; *maybe next year,* I thought.

Following Midnight Mass, we ate warm beignets with hot cocoa; it was difficult to sleep after such excitement.

On Christmas morning, some orphans were assigned to pass the collection baskets at the Cathedral across the street. We were trained to pause and smile whenever we saw young children; magically, the money came pouring into the baskets. Following Mass, the priest rewarded us with chocolate bars. I told the priest that I had three brothers so he gave me four chocolate bars instead of one. Back at the orphanage, I looked for my brothers, and if I didn't see them going up or down the stairs, I gave myself permission to eat all four chocolate bars, sans guilt.

Another holiday favorite was ice-skating with the Sisters. After a good snow, Sister hosed the playground until the snow became a hard, mirror-like surface. I could not wait to get on that ice. I excelled at racing and jumping over hurdles, but I lacked grace when figure skating. Playing hockey games with the Sisters could be aggressive but such fun.

After skating in freezing temperature, my face turned the color of a turnip, and my eye lashes turned to icicles. Once inside, I stood by the furnace till the ice melted from my face, and I stood in a puddle of water. The warmth from the furnace made my whole body tingle.

A favorite holiday snack was lining up with a snow ball on a stick ready to dip in a large pot of hot maple syrup. I watched my snow ball turn into a delicious golden taffy, and I lined up again until the maple syrup ran out.

I am most grateful for the experience of being a guest at Hotel-Dieu where I found self-reliance, worthiness and joy.

How fortunate that I came from Hotel-Dieu, (God's Hotel) and then retired in The Villages, (God's Playground).

Amor Fati, I love my fate!

In Search of Christmas Lost
by
Robert Alan

I knew it was about five minutes before seven because I had just woke up. I have always set my alarm for seven, but for years now I've been waking up at roughly five minutes before seven, just in time to shut the alarm off before it rang. Still, each night I wound the old clock and set the alarm, out of force of habit I guess. I hadn't always awoke before the alarm rang. There was a time when the alarm would run itself out in a vain attempt to be heard over the silence of my sleep. But that was another time, another place, another world.

Times change, people change, and the habits and attitudes that seem to serve us so well in the present, are often altered by the passing years. These changes cannot be, nor should they be, denied. Indeed, they are the very measure by which we mark the passage of time.

The different worlds we pass through in our inexorable journey from birth to death are discreet, and yet at the same time form the continuum that defines our very lives; the innocence of youth, the excitement and confusion of adolescence, the freedom of young adulthood, and the obligations and responsibilities that comes with maturity. Each world with its own set of rules and values, and, when viewed from within, each with a specific yet different understanding of the reality that surrounds us. How strange that one physical world can be perceived in so many different ways.

So it was at five minutes to seven that I got out of bed, neither awake nor asleep, but programmed to prepare myself for work. By seven thirty I was ready to face another day. The sky was clear that morning; the rising sun poured soft yellow light through the tall trees that surrounded my quarters. It was one of those beautiful late spring mornings when everything is in full bloom, but still fresh and shining with morning dew.

Unexpectedly, a sense of attachment stirred within me, as if something was trying to reach out and pull me backwards to another time, another place. Feelings and perceptions from an earlier era in a younger world surreptitiously pushed their way into my consciousness. Then for a brief moment it was there; an awareness of the world as it should be, unencumbered by self-imposed constraints that limit our understanding and appreciation of it. I wanted to somehow grab that feeling, to fix it into my being, to surround myself with this sense of a simpler more benevolent reality. But, as quickly as the epiphany had come, it was gone. Like a meteor streaking across the night sky; we may glimpse it briefly out of the corner of our eye, but when we turn to examine it directly, it vanishes.

Still, this morning held some mysterious fascination for me. I decided to walk to work; it was only a thirty-minute walk, and it would give me time to discover just what this beautiful spring morning was trying to tell me. It was then that I realized it was not spring. It was early December. I had not lived in the temperate south long enough to become accustomed to the mild seasons. Could this really be December? Was it that long ago that December was the month that brought ice and snow, skating and sledding, cranberries and turkey, and best of all the expectations of Christmas?

Way back in the depths of my memory lives a small boy who waits for December like one waits for an old friend. In many ways it was spring then too, and every day brought new life, new lessons, new dreams. Perhaps the spring and the boy and the world they inhabited are still there somewhere in time, but the man who once knew them so well has moved on to winter taking with him only memories.

Every morning from the first of December the little boy woke early, as little boys will do, and very quietly, with restrained excitement and hope, tiptoed through the warm kitchen to the window overlooking a small backyard in a residential neighborhood of a big city. With a smile that shown more from his eyes than his mouth, he would slowly pull back the window shade and peer out into the yard.

Then one morning, after seemingly countless trips to the window, it was there. The light of the new day inched across the boy's face from ear to ear as he eased back the edge of the shade; the smile that was in his eyes spread over his face like an instant sunrise. Snow was still falling in big lazy flakes toward a ground already covered in white. It was an early snow, the kind that clings to fences and the bare branches of sleeping trees; the kind that builds up over the eaves of houses like white ocean waves frozen in time so that they may be enjoyed a little longer. It was still early morning. It would be hours before the children, including the boy, would trample the fluffy snow flat. It would be days before the soot of the city would turn the white to gray. It was this time that the boy liked best; when the whole wonderful white world belonged to him alone. Hurriedly he pulled on his snowsuit, and went out to greet a very new day.

"Hello, Mr. Snow," he said, for a child can speak to almost anything.

Soon snowmen and snow houses were forged out of the white ground, created by a multitude of little hands; the same little hands that later pelted their creations with snowballs. By early afternoon the snow on the side streets had been packed to a hard glossy surface, which made sledding the current in-sport. For hours the squeal of belly-flopping youngsters could be heard, and with each honk of a car horn the squeals stopped, and so did a mother's heart, until the squeals and belly-flops could be hard again. But all days must end, and soon it was time to trade in the wet mittens and leggings for a warm meal and a dry bed. The backyard now bore the scars of the snowball war. The snow houses lie in ruin, the snowmen mortally wounded. But soon new snow would fall, new fortresses would be built, and a new generation of snowmen would rise up from the frozen ground. It was a miracle of snow and ice that renewed itself with each new snowfall, and all the time the bright star of Christmas rose higher in the cold night sky.

In those long ago days there were other signs of the coming of Christmas. The old wooden radio filled the house with Christmas music. Church bells could be heard at all hours chiming "*Silent Night*," "*Noel*," and "*Joy to the World*." On that new invention, *television* could be seen *Dickens' Christmas Carol*, *Frosty the Snowman*, *Rudolph the Red Nosed Reindeer*, and even the birth of Christ. The same stories were shown year after year, but how could one ever grow tired of such stories. Then came that special day when the little boy's mother would say, "*Tomorrow we will go downtown and do our Christmas shopping.*" This was an event to rival Christmas itself, and it meant that Christmas was very near.

The city would be ablaze with lights of every color. Some of the skyscrapers would leave just enough lights on so that from the outside the lighted windows would outline the shape of a star, or an angle. One of the department stores would have a Christmas tree so big you would have to take the escalator to the fourth floor in order to see its top; and in the park there would be an even bigger tree. Store windows would be decorated with the visions of children's dreams, and lamppost would be adorned with Christmas trees, and wreaths, and atop each pole would sit an elf in red and green.

The night finally came and the boy, mother in hand, began his trip to the city. The minutes seemed like hours as they waited on the elevated platform for the train to arrive, but soon a faint rumble was heard in the tracks that quickly grew to a roar and finally to a high-pitched squeal as the train screeched to a halt beside the wooden platform. Then with a clank and grind the elevated train sped off through the night, toward the city. Over the housetops, the back yards, the asphalt parking lots, the train rumbled on its way.

From his vantage point the boy looked down on the streetlights running north and south, east and west; their white light supplemented by the small red and green lights of the season strung between each lamppost. The boy looked down on a giant checkerboard of light, and he was happy. He did not see the tenement houses between the streetlights, with their backyards of concrete surrounded by high wooden or cyclone fences. He did not notice the decaying back porches with their broken railings and rotting stairs. He did not see the children inside who were also waiting for Christmas, a Christmas that would never come.

But we must remember that he is still a child who sees the good in the world because it is the simple and logical thing to see. He does not yet have any reason to suspect a world in which all is not as it should be. In a few years he will take this train ride again, as he does every year; but this time when the train rumbles past the tenements he will see through their soot covered windows a child sitting on the floor for lack of a chair. He will see the porches, the yards, the dimly lit rooms, and he will begin to wonder; and he will begin to understand that his last Christmas is at hand. But for now he sees only what St. Nick himself will see in a couple of nights. The snow covered roofs and yards of a sleeping city.

The train doors opened and the boy walked out onto the elevated wooden platform in the heart of the city. A blaze of colored lights met his eyes, and it was beautiful and exciting as it had been every year since he could remember. A river of people flowed along the sidewalks doing last minute shopping, or just looking into store windows, which told with animated figures the story of '*Rudolph*' or '*Frosty*' or '*Tiny Tim*'. Sounds of Christmas filled the air; the sounds of tambourines, trumpets, and voices from the red and blue clad volunteers of the Salvation Army who sang joyfully and hopefully of the coming of Christ. There were also the sounds of clanging bells held by the men in red and white suits, and white beards, standing beside their red collection buckets; buckets put there to allow people to partake in those unselfish acts of charity, which are so much a part of the Christmas season. How few took advantage of that opportunity, and how loudly the bell rang as you walked by.

Store after store, Toyland after Toyland, the boy and his mother did their Christmas shopping. The stores were decorated with boughs of mistletoe and holly, giant brightly colored ornaments, and flows of angel hair. Christmas music could be heard in the background as people moved from one department to the next buying gifts, and checking off items on their Christmas list.

Much later that night a very tired boy, and an even more tired mother waited on the damp wooden boards of the elevated train station, each holding a large shopping bag filled with brightly wrapped packages. The platform was not crowded; most people had gone home hours ago. It was quiet there, except for those ever present sounds of a big city that usually go unnoticed – the sound of rubber tires rolling along the wet pavement on the street below, the cooing of pigeons as they look for shelter against the raw December weather in the corners and overhangs of buildings, the inevitable honk and counter honk of impatient taxies, and finally the long high-pitched screech of metal against metal as the train grinds to a halt beside the platform.

And so the night had come to an end. The boy sat next to the window munching on a handful of Spanish peanuts he had bought for a penny from a vending machine on the train platform. He was asleep when the train once again rumbled passed the tenements.

One more thing needed doing before Christmas arrived. A Christmas tree had to be found and decorated. For this the boy and his father went out into the cold winter night to one of the few remaining vacant lots in the neighborhood; a vacant lot which around Christmas was transformed into a forest of evergreen. For the boy it was truly a forest – a forest to run in, a forest to hide in, a forest to get lost in, a forest to ambush his father in. New snow had fallen and a soft blanket of white covered the ground, hiding the place where the sawed off trunks of the trees were stuck into holes in the ground. Snow clung to their boughs, and the scent of evergreen filled the air, creating a wilderness in the middle of the city, a wondrous transformation to accompany a wondrous time of year.

Their black rubber boots crunched on the cold dry snow as father and son walked down row after row of trees looking for that one perfect tree they knew must exist somewhere just a little farther into the forest. From the boy's vantage point, he looked up at the dark green trees dusted with sparkling flakes of white, and then farther on to the beautiful winter night sky with its abundance of stars. How clear and bright the stars looked that night. And that one bright star to the left of the Big Dipper; surely that must be the star of Christmas. Oh, what a bright future that star seemed to promise.

Finally a tree was selected, and the forest was diminished by one. By Christmas the forest would once again be a vacant lot.

Mother and Sister greeted Father and Son at the door as they marched triumphantly in with the Christmas tree bound in twine, and riding on their shoulders. Oh, what a night this would be! Every sense took part in the annual decorating of the tree. The smell of popcorn, cinnamon, and hot chocolate filled the air. Boxes were brought down from the attic and opened, revealing a dazzling assortment of colored ornaments, lights, tinsel, garlands of silver, plastic snowmen, paper snowflakes, and a glittering silver star, which the boy himself would place on the top of the tree. No pirate's treasure chest filled with jewels and gold could have brought more excitement than those boxes full of Christmas treasures. Christmas records were played on the old phonograph, and the family sang along as they carefully and deliberately positioned each ornament in just the right place.

Finally the tree was erected and decorated, and absolutely nothing else remained to be done, except to wait for Christmas itself, which was now only a few days away.

It was getting hot by the time I arrived at work. The walk had taken a little longer than thirty minutes, but I guess I had walked slowly that day. Even so, there wasn't enough time to squeeze in Christmas for the boy. However, the boy will have his Christmas without me, as he's been doing ever since we parted so long ago.

But why? Why should Christmas be only for the young? Didn't the promise state, *"peace on earth to all men of good will?"* Didn't this mean people of all ages? Could it be that today Christmas has become too commercial? Maybe so, but the boy's Christmas was also commercial, yet for him the promise of Christmas was fulfilled. From what he could see and understand in his few brief years, which to him seemed like an eternity, there was peace on earth. There was light and joy and love, and therefore no conflict with the joy that should precede the coming of Christ, the coming of hope.

Conflict! Of course, that's it! We try to happily celebrate peace on earth where little exists. While so much light and joy and love are still lacking, we try to celebrate the birth of our redemption. But redemption is a promise of what can be, not what is, or what will be. What will be is up to us.

The gates have been open, but the road to those gates must be traveled using the power of our own free will. We may pray for guidance as we travel that road, and stumble upon those inevitable obstacles over which we have little or no control, but the extent of joy and sorrow that we will encounter along the way is a product of the decisions we all must make as we journey from one waypoint to the next. Whether we believe in the gates or not, the degree of heaven or hell that we experience right here on earth is in large part a consequence our deliberate actions, or perhaps more telling, our inactions. We are, after all, living on a finite planet rife with problems of both natural and manmade origins.

We can choose to work together to overcome these difficulties, or we can choose to go it alone, protecting ourselves from the problems as best we can; or worse yet, just accepting them as unsolvable. It may be that our redemption rests simply in our ability to recognize that there are problems; that civilization itself is still a work in progress. As long as we don't think of ourselves or our institutions as perfect, we leave open the prospect of working toward a better world, a better tomorrow. Our progress has been sluggish, with periods of promising advancement, often followed by periods of disappointing retreat, but there is hope.

Christmas may someday again truly be for people of all ages. All we need do is remove the conflict. All we need ask is that people live in peace, and when called upon, lend a helping hand to those in need. Of course the safety and wellbeing of our families and friends come first, but could we not also, each in our own way, give some measure of comfort and aid to that greater family comprised of all those fellow travelers with whom we share this planet, and with whom we are making this journey? So this is what we must ask of humankind.

Oh my God, will I never see another Christmas.

Time to go to work. I opened the door and walked into the air-conditioned building. It felt good to get out of the hot December sun.

Author Bio:
Robert Alan, a native of Chicago, moved to Panama City, Florida after retiring from the Air Force. He is author of the four-time award winning suspense/thriller novel, *This Way Madness Comes.* Alan's short stories, *Murder*

At Massalina Bayou, and *A Walk in the Park*, appeared in the Florida Writers Association's Collection 5, *It's A Crime Anthology*, and *FWA Collection 6, First Steps Anthology*. Robert's writing interests include both fiction prose and poetry.

Slipper's Last Breath
by
John D. Ottini

It's the day before Christmas, a time of happiness and joy, but in my heart I know this Christmas will not be a joyful occasion.

The fireplace crackles and pops as my eyes are drawn to the front window, where large and fluffy snowflakes fall, covering the trees and yard. Tears build in my eyes, but I dare not allow them escape, in fear that they will not stop once they begin flowing. In need of distraction, I switch the radio on, and the joyous sound of Christmas music fills the room. For a few moments my spirit is lifted and my thoughts drift to happier times.

I take a sip of hot coffee and half-heartedly continue placing ornaments on the tree. Decorating the Christmas tree has never been one of my strong points, but I promised my wife, Mary, that every Christmas I would decorate the tree in her honor, until the day we met again.

It's been five long years since she's been gone, and yet I still see her face, smell the scent of her hair, and crave her gentle touch. I've lived 63 years without serious illness, but in the last few years, I've battled through my share of pain and heartache. When Mary was diagnosed with pancreatic cancer, I couldn't catch my breath for three days. As the months went by, and the treatment became worse than the illness, I knew that her pain and mine would never go away.

When she passed away, my world was shattered. My wife, best friend, lover, and soul mate was gone, and so was my reason for living. Retired, alone and depressed, each day was a struggle to survive. There were days when I couldn't find a single reason to get out of bed. I know that Mary would be upset to see me this way, but nothing made me happy.

Mary and I never had children, but fortunately our friends and family did the best they could to keep me busy moving forward, and in time I began to heal. Now when I think back on that difficult time, I realize that no one was more instrumental in keeping me sane and alive than our cat, Slipper.

Slipper was twelve when Mary died, and that poor tabby wandered around the house for days, searching for her best friend, wondering where she had gone. At the time, I could not imagine what she was going through, grieving over the loss of her companion, because I was far too busy drowning in my own sorrow to pay attention to her needs. I fed Slipper and cleaned her litter, but other than that, I was totally numb to her existence.

As you may have surmised, Slipper was Mary's baby; I was just the guy who competed for Mary's attention, and on occasion accidently stepped on her tail. We got along okay, but we were never close, and we certainly weren't best buddies.

After her death, it took a good six months for Slipper to feel comfortable occupying the same room as me. At nine months she allowed me to pet her and would sometimes curl up in my lap on cold winter evenings. On rare occasions when I left the house, she would be waiting for me at the front window and would greet me with meows and leg rubs at the door. At night she would sleep at the foot of the bed and wake me each morning by walking on my chest and licking my nose. At first the routine annoyed me, but eventually I found comfort in the attention she gave me every morning. On the odd occurrence when she didn't wake me up in this manner, I worried that something might be wrong, but it was usually nothing, and I would find her staring out the window at some rabbit or squirrel.

At the one year mark, we were indeed the best of friends.

Now, I cannot imagine my day without her brushing against my leg, jumping on the newspaper, or playing hide-and-seek. She is a very vocal companion and has no trouble letting me know when she wants my attention or when it's mealtime. I've always considered myself a tough guy, but I know without a doubt that I love my cat and that she is the focal point of my life.

I stare across the room, and the smile evaporates from my face. She lies quietly on her favorite pillow in front of the fire place, staring back at me, her eyes following my every move. At seventeen years of age, her vision is failing; her coat is no longer shiny or well-groomed, and her energy level is almost nonexistent. It takes something very special to get the old girl off her pillow and prancing across the room. When she does move, it's always in a slow and cautious manner, her way of hiding the pain of her illness.

Recent visits to the veterinarian's office did not bring us good news. The vet informed me that she had developed feline leukemia and

40

that her days on this earth were numbered. At her age, there was not much he could do medically, so he suggested that I do my best to keep her as comfortable and happy as possible.

I know that the inevitable is coming, but Slipper is my last connection to Mary, and I'm finding it very difficult to say goodbye.

I walk over to the fireplace and sit down beside her. She looks up at me with her sad, brown eyes and purrs softly as I pet her. Her body feels cold, and her once beautiful coat is no longer soft and glossy.

"Hello baby, how are you feeling today?"

She just stares back at me.

"Girl, I would do anything to make you feel better. I hope you know that."I whisper as my throat goes dry. "I have no idea what I will do without you, my friend."

She looks at me as if to say, *"It's okay Dad, I'm still here, don't be sad, I'll be fine if you'll be fine . . . I'm not afraid."*

Moisture fills in my eyes and a lump develops in my throat. I know that I have to let her go, but it's more difficult than I ever imagined.

"I'm right here girl; don't be afraid. I don't want you to suffer any more", I tell her as I gently touch her nose. Her nose is dry and rough, but it is still the cutest little nose I have ever seen.

"Don't worry about me, I'll be okay." I lied to the best of my ability.

"Are you sure Dad? Do you promise you will be okay? I can't leave knowing you won't be okay without me."

Be strong, I keep telling myself. Let her know that it's alright to say goodbye. I smile bravely, stroke the soft spot above her nose, and nod my head in approval. She takes one last look at me and lays her head on my lap; then she closes her eyes and takes her last breath.

My body begins to tremble, and the tears roll down my cheeks. I hug and kiss Slipper on the forehead and cover her in her favorite blanket. I grab my coat and step out into the cold air, but there is no escaping the unbearable ache inside my heart. My body slides down the wall, and I cry uncontrollably. Why did this have to happen on Christmas Eve?

I don't remember how long I've been crying, but I feel the cold numbness in my hands, and I know I have to get to a warmer place. I can't bear going back into the house, so I run to my car and slip behind the wheel. A feeling of absolute loneliness consumes me; it's as if Mary has died all over again. If I have to go through this one more time, I don't think I will survive.

I jam the keys in the ignition, start the engine and back out of the driveway. I have to speak to someone, and I know who that someone is. I crank up the heater and pull out onto State Road 10, then drive 10 miles south to Mission Valley Road, where I turn right onto Old Cemetery Road. The old car has finally warmed up, but I am so consumed with the thought of telling Mary that Slipper is gone, I hardly notice that my hands are no longer cold.

The cemetery sidewalk is buried in snow, but I manage to shuffle through until I reach my Mary's gravesite. I brush the afternoon snow from the tombstone to reveal Mary's photograph and her epitaph etched in stone.

MARY BELSON MASTERSON
1950 - 2009
BELOVED WIFE OF WILLIAM MASTERSON
A precious one from us has gone.
A voice we loved is stilled.
A place is vacant in our hearts, which never can be filled.
Until we meet again.

After all these years, I still get choked up every time I visit her grave. Today I fall to my knees, look to the sky, and feel the icy snowflakes land on my face.

"Hello sweetheart, it's me, Bill. I came here to let you know that your baby, Slipper, passed away today and is coming home to see you."

A cold wind blows through the cemetery, followed by what sounds like a painful scream. Momentarily shocked, I glance around, but I see no one. I am alone. I place a hand over my mouth when I realize that the sound had involuntarily escaped from my throat in my moment of grief.

"She passed away quietly at home on her favorite pillow. I don't think she suffered much, but I miss her already."

Warm tears flow down my cheeks. I raise my collar up to keep the chill from my neck, but nothing brings me warmth or comfort at this moment of despair. I feel lost and distraught; everyone I love in this world is gone.

"My love, I promised you I would continue on without you that I would try to be happy until we meet again, but I don't think I have the strength to go on like this. How do I know you are even listening to me?

How can I be sure that I will ever see you and Slipper again? I'm alone Mary, so alone in this world."

Mary hated when I questioned my faith. She never understood why I couldn't just believe and be happy. I had always wished I had that kind of strength and belief in the concept of everlasting life, but I didn't. One day, I remember asking her why she believed so strongly in the afterlife, since there is no way to prove its existence?

Her reply shocked me, "Because the alternative is too sad and frightening to imagine."

"My love, I miss you so much and I love you with all my heart. Please send me a sign, any sign, which will help me to believe that my life is still worth living!"

I hear a car door slam behind me and the sound of children's voices echo through the cemetery. Upset and shaken, I get up off my knees, brush the snow off my pants, blow a kiss to Mary, and head to the car. In the automobile, I begin having serious thoughts about committing suicide. There is no point of living in a constant state of misery!

It is 5:30 p.m. and dusk has turned to night. I switch on the headlights and start home. I decide at that moment that I will have Slipper's body cremated right after the holidays and will scatter her ashes over Mary's grave. It will be the closest thing to a reunion they will ever have, and I know that it will please Mary. Once that is done, I will deal with myself.

A short time later I pull into the driveway, switch off the engine and sit in silence. I hear the ticking and clicking noises as the engine cools down. I wonder if I can go back into that house without having a complete mental breakdown. I sit awhile longer, trying to motivate myself to go inside, but in the end it's the thought of freezing to death in the car that sends me heading toward the front door.

As I reach the door, I can hear Josh Groban singing *Oh Holy Night*, and my heart sinks. I don't want to be alone on Christmas Eve, especially not this Christmas Eve. My fingers are stiff from the cold, and I drop my keys while trying to unlock the door. I reach down to pick them up and hear a soft, scratching sound coming from inside the front door.

"What the heck is that?" I say out loud. I listen and hear it again. I open the door slowly, not knowing what to expect, and there at the door stands Slipper staring at me. I stand frozen, unable to move, a look of disbelief on my face, and then she lets out a deep and loud meow.

I'm not sure what it means, but I'm guessing she said, "Come in and close the damn door. It's cold outside". I pick her up and hug her, as my heart explodes with love. I laugh and I'm dancing around the room, like an idiot, then I begin crying, but this time they are tears of pure joy.

"How can this be?" I said out loud. "I don't understand how this is possible?"

Slipper licks my face and looks at me as if to say, *"Dad, don't ask how or why, just be as happy as I am, that we have each other one last time for Christmas."*

"You're right, girl," I said as I kissed her on the nose and told her I loved her. "You are so right."

Then it hits me, this is my sign? My one last gift from Mary and Slipper? My true Christmas miracle?

I pour myself a cup of coffee, and Slipper a small saucer of milk. Then we sit quietly enjoying each other's company and listening as the holiday music brings forth another Christmas morning. It is one of the happiest moments of my life.

Two days go by and our beloved Slipper passes away in her sleep, and as promised, I am at the cemetery scattering her ashes over Mary's grave.

As I drive away, I realize that Slipper has once again saved my life. I don't know for certain what brought her back to me when I needed her most, but I know that I am no longer sad and depressed. I now believe that my loved ones are together forever, and that one day soon, I too will see them again.

After all, the alternative is indeed too sad and frightening to imagine.

Author Bio:

John D. Ottini was born in Northern Italy, raised and educated in Canada and now resides in Central Florida, with his wife Nancy and a mischievous cat named Bella.

John has published three mystery novels, *My Journey to Hell*, *A Fool and His Money* and his latest, *The Object of Your Desire*. All are available from the Amazon Kindle Store.

Follow John at his Blog – www.jdonovels.wordpress.com

Gabriel
by
Gerry Wolfson-Grande

Ben Fisher glanced around the empty kitchen, then spotted his son on the deck, staring at the gray December sky. Ben poured them coffee and slipped outside.

"Are you all right?"

"Yeah, I'm fine." Tom sounded unconvincing. He had just finished up a long, punishing case; his eyes were dull, trenches of shadows dug underneath them.

"You look terrible. When did you last get a decent night's sleep?"

Tom scrubbed a hand over his face.

"Just post-case resolution, Dad."

"Why don't you take some time off? A vacation even."

"You mean like you haven't taken for the last several years?"

They both laughed, then Tom's smile faded.

"Okay, son. Out with it."

Tom sighed.

"Dad – have you ever had times when you wonder if you're doing the right thing?"

His father gave him a sharp look, and he added, "With your life, I mean."

Ben said nothing, waiting.

"I think I'm burning out, Dad."

"Because of this last case?"

"No. It's everything. Guns and shootings in school; the neighbors massacred because someone cut down the wrong tree; drivers blowing each other away; parents abandoning their kids, families disintegrating – nobody cares about anyone else anymore. I'm starting to wonder if I'm doing anyone one damn bit of good trying to hold things together."

This was more than the occasional griping about his job; the weariness and discouragement were new. Ben struggled, searching for the right words.

"None of us can save the world singlehandedly," he finally said. "We can only try to influence our small corner of it. The point is, you care about what you do. I think you'll be able to acknowledge that, once you've gotten some rest."

"I don't know." Tom shook his head again. "I'm not sure that I do care anymore." His phone beeped. "Gotta go, Dad. Don't worry, I'll be okay."

Tom frowned as Denny's text message canceled their meeting. Grumbling, he started down the deserted street towards his car, pulling up his jacket collar against the wind. It was unusually chilly for this early in December, and he was cold. Just one more thing wrong with the world; everything going to hell or worse. Distracted, he failed to notice the boy until a small body cannoned into him.

"Whoa! What's your rush, kid?"

Tom picked the boy up and looked him over, wondering what crime scene was being abandoned.

Huge brown eyes blinked up at him.

"Please, mister, it's my mom. She needs help."

Letting the boy pull him into a dilapidated building nearby, Tom saw a young woman lying on blankets on the floor, a meager collection of possessions and makeshift furnishings nearby. He dropped to his knees beside her.

"Ma'am? My name's Tom Fisher. I'm a police officer. Can you tell me what happened?"

"Police?" She glanced around her pitiful homestead, and he rushed to reassure her.

"It's all right. Just tell me your name, and what happened, so I can help."

"Mary Davidson. I'm not sure what happened. I was dizzy – and then I must have fallen – no, Nathan helped me lie down."

Tom sat back on his heels. "Good kid. How old are you, Nathan?"

"I'm six. Are you going to help my mom?"

"Yes, I am. My car's just up the street. I'm going to take you to Community Memorial; my dad's chief of staff there, and he'll take good care of you."

"Hospital?" she protested feebly. "But what about our things?"

So little, and so inadequate, to consider one's own and important. "Don't worry. I'll make sure they're taken care of." He rose, helping her up. "Here, lean on me, unless you'd rather I carried you."

"No, thank you, I can manage."

As Nathan scooted ahead, Tom heard an ominous crack, and he felt the floorboard beneath his right foot starting to sag. He started to push Mary clear, but he was too late, and a large portion of flooring gave way, taking victim and rescuer with it.

He couldn't have been out long. Tom looked around to orient himself, wishing his head would clear. They seemed to be caught somewhere in the subflooring, but the pain in his chest – broken ribs, probably – kept him from moving to check. Mary was lodged just above him to his right, her left leg clearly broken. He fished for his phone.

"Hang on, Mary," he muttered, as Nathan yelled hysterically from above.

"Mom! Tom! Are you okay?"

It hurt to breathe, much less talk, but Tom called upwards anyway, anxious to calm the child. "Don't worry, Nathan. Your mom's leg's broken, but otherwise she's fine. I'm going to call 911. The paramedics will be here right away."

His phone looked like his ribs felt. Its face was cracked, and it had no dial tone. Tom craned his neck, making eye contact with the boy.

"Nathan, I need you to go to the nearest phone and dial 911. Tell them where we are. Can you do that, buddy?"

The boy's eyes widened.

"But you said – "

"I'm afraid his cell phone's broken, honey," Mary said. "Don't worry, we'll be all right. Just run down to the drugstore on the corner and tell them what's happened; and they'll call the hospital.

Hurry, sweetie. I love you."

"Okay, Mom. I love you too." Then he ran off.

Tom turned to apologize to the woman he was supposed to be rescuing. She had drifted off again, and she seemed to be blurring around the edges. He was puzzling over this when he felt a trickle of liquid slide down his forehead; when he touched it, his fingers came away blood-stained. That explains it, he thought, just before he lost consciousness as well.

"Tom Fisher, can you hear me?"

"Yes." His head and ribs hurt.

"My name's Gabe, Gabriel DiAngelo. I'm an EMT. I'm here to help you."

He didn't hear anyone else.

"Where's …" Tom started, gasping as another lightning bolt went through his aching temples.

Amazingly, Gabriel understood.

"They're on their way. I was near when the call came in."

"Mr. DiAngelo…"

"Gabe," the other man said. "Tom, I need you to tell me how secure those floorboards feel, so I can get you two out of there."

Secure wasn't even close. "I don't think three of us down here would be a very good idea."

"Okay. Can you reach Mrs. Davidson?"

Wondering how the EMT knew both their names took too much energy; he stopped trying and carefully stretched out one arm, then the other, ignoring protests from his ribs. "Yeah."

"Good. Now reach towards me so I can see where you are. Okay. I saw some wood by the wall. I'm going to get a couple of pieces for a splint. Don't go anywhere."

Ordinarily, Tom would have been irritated, but there was something so relaxed, so confident, so reassuring about this guy.

"We'll try not to wander off."

Footsteps moved away above his head, and returned, accompanied by a child's voice.

"Okay," Gabriel said. "Nathan, we're going to hand these pieces of wood down to Lt. Fisher."

Maybe the kid had given their names during the 911 call, but Tom hadn't mentioned his rank. He opened his mouth, but was distracted by one, then two pieces of wood swimming downward. He snagged them without upsetting his ribs too much, and glanced across at Mary.

"I'll hold those for you, Tom."

"Good, you're awake," Gabriel said. "Mrs. Davidson, we're going to splint your leg, and the paramedics are coming. Are you okay otherwise?"

"I'll be all right."

"Tom, strapping's coming your way," Gabriel continued. "Mary, if you'll hold those pieces in place, Tom can secure them."

Did DiAngelo just carry the stuff around with him? *Another puzzle to shelve temporarily*, Tom thought, concentrating on wrapping it around the slats. The paramedics arrived just as he finished, the pounding in his head adding a rhythm track to the chorus of pain shrieking through his ribs. Soon he and Mary were lying on stretchers, their injuries being tended.

A face floated into his line of sight. It was not young, but it seemed untouched by life, with none of the customary bits and pieces of facial road map which come with age. Its features were beautiful, androgynous even, a definitive masculinity nevertheless in the chiseled line of nose, jaw and brow. Dark reddish-brown, almost black curls tumbled over forehead, ears, and the nape of the neck. And there was something about the eyes – Tom stared at them, feeling foggier. Then Gabriel spoke, and the odd feeling of otherwhereness eased.

"They're about to transport you. I'd like to follow along if you don't mind."

No, he didn't mind. He had a few questions. Tom started to speak, but it came out in an indistinct mumble.

Gabriel was one step ahead of him again.

"Don't sweat it, Tom. I'll see you later."

Then the cool darkness closed in, welcoming him.

Ben was in his office when his phone rang.

"Ben Fisher."

It was Colin Matthews in the ER.

"Ben, they just brought Tom in. Don't panic. He's going to be okay, but I thought you might want to see him before I start doing things to him."

"I'll be right down."

The young doctor was leaning over his friend's gurney, checking Tom's eyes and gently probing the head wound, as Ben came in.

"Looks like the damage was limited to a gash over his forehead, not very deep, cuts and scrapes, three broken ribs, mild concussion. As usual, I'm getting films to be on the safe side."

Tom's eyelids fluttered at the familiar touch.

"Colin?"

"You're going to be fine, buddy. I just want a closer look at those ribs, and then we'll get you fixed up. In the meantime, you're going to take a nice little nap."

"Wait. The woman – Mary...?"

"She's going to be okay. She's in x-ray right now."

"There was something wrong..."

Ben caught Colin's eye as the younger doctor started to insert a syringe into the IV. "What do you mean, Tom?"

"She...she was sick when I got there." A pause while he concentrated, then Tom added, "She said she was dizzy. I was...bringing her out when..."

Ben nodded at Colin.

"We'll take care of it, son. You need to rest."

"But..."

Colin pressed the plunger for the IV.

"But nothing, buddy. Tell your ribs to smile for the camera and say night-night."

Father and best friend watched as Tom's breathing slowed and deepened. Finally, Colin took a deep breath.

"Mrs. Davidson should be back from x-ray by now."

Ben nodded. "Think I'll come meet her. Do we know what happened?"

"Not exactly. The paramedics said an EMT was already there when they arrived, but I haven't seen him yet. All I know is Tom and the woman had fallen through rotting floorboards and were trapped. Her son went to the nearest store and called 911."

"Son?"

"Yes. Nathan; six years old. Lizbeth's taking care of him. Let's go see if his mother's back."

Looking at Mary's films, Ben commented, "Looks like a fairly clean break of the left tibia; the paramedics did a good splinting job."

"Your son did that mostly."

A youngish man was standing in the doorway.

"Gabe DiAngelo. I heard the call go in, and went to help until the crew got there."

Ben shook the proffered hand.

"Ben Fisher. You said Tom...?"

"He and Mrs. Davidson were stuck in a rather precarious spot, and he didn't think it was going to support us all. So I worked the materials down to him, and he splinted her leg."

Gabriel's strangely light eyes focused on Ben, who experienced an odd feeling of weightlessness before the other man spoke again.

"I'd say you could be proud of your son, except I believe you already know that."

Startled, Ben nodded.

"Yes, I do...and I am − even if sometimes he doubts his own abilities."

Colin coughed, and Gabriel focused on him.

"Actually, Dr. Matthews, I stopped in to see Tom, but I'd also like to visit Mary Davidson as well."

"Once we get her leg set, sure. She just came back from x-ray, so give me about a half hour."

"Okay. Doctors, I'll catch up with you later."

As Gabriel left, Colin asked, "Did you notice anything…well, strange…about him?"

"No…at least I think I didn't."

Colin gave him a sharp look, but Ben didn't elaborate. The fluorescent lighting in the hospital had been known to play tricks on the eyes before, probably accounting for the glow he thought he had seen around Gabriel's head. He took a breath, rubbed his eyes, and glanced over at Ben.

"Ready to get Mary's story?"

Mary Davidson smiled drowsily at the two doctors.

"Dr. Fisher, is your son all right?"

"He's a bit banged up and sore, but he'll be fine, thank you. And our Dr. Lizbeth Kelly is looking after Nathan."

"Why were you living in that building?" Colin asked. "The neighborhood's basically condemned."

She sighed.

"We just came here a week ago. The furniture-making company where we lived went bankrupt last month. It was a one-industry town; everyone lost everything.. So we came here, but we couldn't find a place to stay. We were driving around…it was late, and we had to sleep. And Joseph…"

"Where is your husband, Mrs. Davidson?" Ben asked.

Tears started in her eyes.

"I don't know. He left the day before yesterday to look for work, but he didn't come back…what if he returns while we're here? He won't know where we are!"

"Relax," Colin soothed. "We'll make sure that someone keeps an eye out for him."

"Already arranged." Gabriel stood in the doorway, looking like a perfectly ordinary EMT to Colin's eyes. "How are you feeling, Mrs. Davidson?"

"Better, I think. But I'm worried about what was making me dizzy."

"We'll find out," Colin said. "But you need to rest."

"True," Gabriel agreed. "You should start conserving your energy now."

"What do you mean, now?" Ben asked.

Gabriel looked at Mary. "You didn't know either."

"Know what?" she asked.

Gabriel gave an odd little half shrug, and smiled, the light eyes even clearer.

"You're going to have a baby."

"How do you know?" Colin demanded.

Gabriel's phone beeped. "Please excuse me. Mary, do what these nice doctors tell you; I'll be back later." He left, leaving two baffled physicians and an equally puzzled patient.

"Very interesting young man," Ben remarked. "Ever see him before today?"

"No. He must have a different run." Colin stared off after Gabriel then turned to his patient. "We'll check your blood, but if you're pregnant, you're not very far along at all, Mary."

"Maybe we should try to locate Mr. Davidson," Ben said. "Do you know where he was going, Mary?"

"I think over in Hollywood."

"What's he look like?"

She smiled.

"Nice. Solid…like a teddybear…I'm sorry, I suppose a more practical description would be helpful."

"Just a little," Colin deadpanned.

"Tom gets cranky when we expect too many miracles."

"I do not." Tom had rolled up in a wheelchair, IV rolling along behind.

Mary smiled at him. "Lt. Fisher, I can't thank you enough for what you did."

Tom looked uncomfortable, and his father rescued him.

"Mary was giving us a description of her husband."

"Yes. Joseph's 5'10", 180 pounds. Light brown hair, mustache and beard. Not too thick."

"Age? Clothes?"

"Thirty-one. He was wearing chinos, a blue striped shirt, blue tie, navy blazer, and loafers."

Colin asked, "What color are his eyes?"

"Hazel."

"Excuse me." Colin took off at a run. Returning, he whispered in Ben's ear. Ben's eyebrows flew up, and both men left. After a few minutes, they were back.

"I'd still like to know how he did it," Colin muttered. "Mary, your bloodwork came back."

"He was right? I'm pregnant? Another baby! Oh, wait till Joseph…"

Then the tears started again.

Ben took her hand.

"Honey, there's more. I think we know where Joseph is."

"Actually," Colin added, "I think he's that John Doe you've been trying to track down for us, Tom."

"What?" Mary cried.

"This guy was brought in two evenings ago after his taxi was sideswiped," Colin told her. "He's not critical, but he took a knock on the head and he's been pretty confused. No ID, so we've been keeping him for observation until we could find out who he is…and I think we have."

The small family soon was reunited in Mary's room.

Tom and Colin watched in companionable silence as the trio hugged and exclaimed over each other. Finally, Tom stirred.

"Good work, Colin," he remarked.

His best friend raised an eyebrow.

"I could say the same about you, Tom."

Ben came up behind them.

"I hate to break up your mutual admiration society, but Tom's going back to his room for a rest before I even think about releasing him to go home."

Someone or something was observing him. Tom looked up as Gabriel walked into his room.

"How are you feeling, Tom?"

"Sore. Stiff. Wiser about wandering through abandoned buildings."

Gabriel laughed, then sobered.

"Not about why you were there in the first place, I hope."

"No…I…Why am I telling you this, anyway?" Tom fumbled for words, then remembered one of his questions. "Gabe, how did you know my name? And my rank?"

Gabriel looked startled.

"Nathan must have said, or I heard it on the call."

"I never told Nathan, or his mother, that I'm a lieutenant, just that I was a police officer."

Gabriel shrugged.

"No idea. Maybe he just assumed." He laughed at Tom's expression. "Tom, I don't read minds."

"But…"

"My friend, listen to me. Detective or no, there are more important things in this world than how I knew your name."

"I don't like unsolved mysteries."

The strange eyes focused on him. "Tom, you have more important concerns worrying you than anything to do with me."

"Such as?"

"Holding it together. Doing your job, doing it well no matter what, knowing what you do is necessary and does make a difference."

This was weird. His father wouldn't have told this guy…no.

"What do you mean?"

Gabriel smiled down at him.

"Today, despite putting yourself in harm's way, you preserved a woman's life and reunited a family. Maybe you haven't saved the whole world yet, but you saved theirs."

Now he remembered what he had seen earlier. Gabriel's eyes were unusually light and clear for a man with his coloring. And eyes that translucent should have reflected something, but Tom only saw bottomless depths, making him feel dizzy.

"Who are you?"

Gabriel said nothing. Instead, he pressed Tom's shoulder and smiled at him again, then started to leave.

"Wait. Who are you? And why…"

"You know the answers to your questions. Both of them. All of them. I just helped you look in the right direction. Fare well."

As Gabriel turned away, the lights flickered. Tom rubbed his eyes; when he looked, the doorway was empty.

Colin and Lizbeth were talking by the nurses' station when Ben appeared with his son.

"You're letting him go home?"

Tom made a face.

"No meatloaf tonight. At least there's beer at home."

They all laughed, then Ben said, "You can stay another day if you need the down time, you know."

"Thanks, Dad, but I think I'm okay now. It took a couple of strangers to help me put things back into perspective, is all."

"I just checked in on the Davidsons," Colin reported. "Joseph may be able to go back to work in a week or so."

"And," Lizbeth added, "I have a friend who's looking for a skilled cabinetmaker, so I think Joseph will have a job before Christmas."

"Good thing," Tom remarked. "Their family's going to get bigger soon."

"You know," Ben mused, "we never did find out how Gabriel knew that."

"Maybe we should ask," Lizbeth said. "Isn't that him over by the elevators?"

Ben turned.

"Gabe!" he called.

Gabriel looked up, waved, and vanished.

Ben whirled to face the others. "Did you see what I saw?"

"That's strange," Lizbeth said, pointing at the desk calendar. "Look what day it is today."

"December 8th," Ben said. "I'll be…"

"The Annunciation," Lizbeth added. "I don't believe it."

"And?" Colin asked.

Ben looked pensive.

"The day an angel came to give a young woman, and the whole world, some news that would change them forever."

There was a sudden stillness, in a building which ordinarily contained so much hustle and bustle, sounds of beeping machinery and efficient personnel. Then the lights flickered, and Lizbeth swore later she had felt something soft brush against her face, as had the others; then the usual sounds of the hospital started up again, and they were back in the normal world, each left to wonder just what had happened…just a little.

Author Bio:

Gerry Wolfson-Grande, writer, editor, paralegal, and musician, grew up in the Washington, D.C., area, with the exception of five years in Germany, and eventually settled in Orlando, Florida. A. graduate of Rollins College (BA in history and MA in Liberal Studies) in Winter Park, Florida, her first published short story, *Not a Good Night at Ford's,* was published first in *Pulse Magazine* and then in *Under the Cosmic Sofa* (Partners in Crime, 2009). It also won an FWA Royal Palm Literary Award. Other publications include *Like,* in *Pets*

Across America, (2011); *My Wheels Have Names*, in *Wheels* (FWA anthology 2012); and *The Chess Players,* in *Slices of Life* (FWA anthology 2010). The *Chess Players,* first story in Gerry's novel-in-stories, *The Chess Players*, was written as part of her graduate work and is currently being revised for commercial publication. *Lillian McNab and the Gerbil of Doom,* a Halloween short story, evolved from a friendly dare by a friend who, like Gerry, couldn't resist the idea of a story with a Gerbil of Doom in it.

The Christmas Present
by
Joan West

Ted Mira didn't look the way you might imagine a terrorist would look. He looked like a lawyer or doctor or the journalist that he pretended to be. In fact, he was an out-of-work actor with a chip on his shoulder. He had been recruited by a terrorist cell to blow up Maxie's, a popular restaurant in the center of the city.

"Why Maxie's?" He had asked. "Why not City Hall?"

"We'll get to City Hall, but that's what everyone expects, chump. What's going to get some action is to do the unexpected." The contact man threw back his head and laughed. "Think of it ... everybody running around crying about all the *innocent* people who were killed and on their holy day ... Christmas!" His laughter stopped. "Innocent! Infidels! ... All of them."

"I don't care who they are as long as I get paid," Ted said.

"You'll get what's coming to you. Just don't screw up."

Ted had studied two small electronic devices the contact man had given him, each no bigger than a large spool of thread. One, when detonated by pushing a button on the other, would cause an explosion powerful enough to flatten Maxie's and the whole city block around it.

He had devised a plan. He would meet a woman, invite her to Christmas dinner at Maxie's, manage to secrete the device in her handbag, and leave her in the restaurant, while he drove away and pushed the magic button. Piece of pie ... He had already reserved a table for the big day.

After a couple of strike-outs, he met Marion at a church social. He had thought of going to a bar, but decided the greatest irony would be to do the job through a "true believer." It hadn't been difficult to persuade her. This was her first time alone in the city on Christmas, far away from her family and friends in the mid-west.

He'd played the lonely bachelor and told her how he hated to eat and do things like going to movies alone and now to have to spend Christmas alone was the worst of all. Inviting her to share Christmas dinner with him at an upscale restaurant like Maxie's had sealed her fate. "…and, we'll go to a movie first. White Christmas is playing at the Rialto. I could see that a dozen times over. How about it?"

"I was great, I could have won a Tony," he said to his reflection in the mirror as the electric razor glided over his handsome face on Christmas morning.He was ready. All he had to do was put the small electronic device in her handbag while they were at the movie; then let her out in front of the restaurant while he parked the car. When he was safely away, he would push the button and *bang*, Maxie's and the cloying Marion would be history.

"Marion, it's good to see you again," he said on Christmas day after she was seated in his sleek silver convertible.
"I'm glad to see you, too, Ted. Merry Christmas."
"Yeah, Merry Christmas." He hesitated before starting the car's engine. "That's one big handbag you have. It's practically a suitcase," he said. "Let me put it behind the seat for you."
"No. It's fine. I'll just put it on the floor by my feet."
In the movie, she held the handbag firmly in her lap. In the lobby after the movie, he offered to hold it for her when she went into the restroom.
"Thanks, but I need to refresh my lipstick," she said.
He was beginning to panic. It was time to go to Maxie's and he hadn't found an excuse to slip the device into her bag. If worse came to worse, he decided, he could accompany her into the restaurant, find a chance to drop the device in the bag, and excuse himself on the pretext of going to the men's room.
Then his luck seemed to change. In the theater parking lot, Marion agreed that the bag was large and unwieldy and that she might be more comfortable with it in the back seat. His hand was in his pocket fingering the device, when…
"Ted! How are you? Where have you been keeping yourself?"
It was the voice of his friend, Martin, a fellow actor. Ted was forced to remove his hand from his pocket, when Martin extended his. After being introduced to Marion and engaging in pleasantries for a few minutes, Martin finally left, but it too late for Ted to reach into the handbag without her noticing it.
What to do? He couldn't fake the need to make a phone call. She knew he had his cell phone in his pocket. Cigarettes! That might do it.

"I hope you won't mind if we make a slight detour. There's a drugstore not too far from here that's open today, and I need a pack of cigarettes."

"I didn't know you smoked," she said.

"I don't really, but I do enjoy a cigarette with coffee after a good meal." He knew that a gentleman would ask if the smoke would bother her, but he was only pretending to be a gentleman and, if he asked and she objected, his last chance, short of going into the restaurant with her, would be gone.

He emerged from the drugstore with a carton of lights.

"That's an awful lot of cigarettes for just one after dinner."

"It's cheaper this way," he explained and walked around to her side of the car, taking a pack out and putting it in his jacket pocket, slipping the device out at the same time. "I'll just put these under your handbag," he said.

Mission accomplished. He got back into the car smiling, and reached over to pat her hand.

"It was a good movie," he said, "And it's going to be an even better dinner."

She returned his smile. "I'm looking forward to it," she said.

You don't know the half of it, he thought, swinging the car out into the traffic. *You don't know the half of it.*

Within minutes, they were in front of the restaurant.

"Don't get out," she said. "There's too much traffic. I'll wait for you in the lobby."

Marion walked across the pavement in front of Maxie's and as the doorman held the door open for her, she stopped. "I forgot my handbag," she said aloud, and turned back toward the street, but it was too late. Ted was already pulling away.

A block and a half away from Maxie's, Ted smiled thinking about how clever he had been. "Goodbye, sweetheart. Thanks for the use of the handbag," he said and pushed the detonator button.

Author Bio:

Following a career as a college professor, Joan West was a founding partner in the Bennett & West Literary Agency. Later, along with her partner, Lois Bennett, she founded Fireside Publications. Now retired, she devotes herself to writing, gardening, traveling and enjoying life in Central Florida with husband Glen. Her most recent work is *Disappearing Daisies: An Ellen Kerry Mystery.*

A Stitch in Time

by
Alison Neuman

My Mom grew up in a different time. Her parents, my Grandma and Grandpa, immigrated to Canada in the early 1900's where the family acquired a farm to provide for their livelihood.

Mom grew up on that farm, and the stories she told me were of her life during those times. The family grew food in the fields and would preserve it by canning it to last over the long cold Alberta winters. An important part of their family was their milking cow, who provided their family with dairy products to sustain them. Water collected from a local creek was boiled in order for them to have warm water for washing and cooking. Heat was maintained with a stove and light was provided by the sun and candles. Extra warmth was achieved with the use of quilts and bed sheets that Grandma sewed with the fabric they purchased when, on the rare occasion, they would take the horses and journey into town.

Pillowcases and table cloths were decorated with embroidered flowers, and when it was for a specific person's room, included an animal or flower of the person's preference. Mom told me how she and Grandma would sit in the winter evenings, by the light of the candles and talk and sew. My Grandma had sewn me a Raggedy Ann doll with beautiful orange embroidered hair. When I was young, I wanted to learn embroidery like my Mom and Grandma.

As soon as I was old enough, Mom taught me how to embroidery. Due to having developed onset *dermatomyositis* when I was a little over three years old, arthritis was attempting to steal the mobility from my fingers, but that was not going to stop me. We sat by the dining room table, during cold wintery evenings, with heat from our furnace and light from our ceiling fan. Mom and I chatted as she sewed an intricate lace pattern on a delicate handkerchief. I used an old pillowcase in a hoop as my location for a simple pink flower.

I generally ignored the potential distractions offered by television, music, and books, as I learned and was inspired by Mom. I found being able to create something with my own two hands was gratifying, but more than the items we were creating, was an opportunity to spend with my hero and my best friend. Through many years, Mom and I were able to spend time making various homemade and personalized gifts that could not have been purchased in any store.

While attending junior high school, Home Economics was my first choice for an elective class, so I could attempt to learn how to sew while still getting my required credits. Mom could not only design patterns but she sewed the most beautiful dresses for myself and clothes for my dolls. She was my mentor and inspiration as I learned the intricacies of hand sewing, patterns, materials, threads, threading a machine, and project planning.

My projects ranged from a pizza shaped pillow, to a mouse pin cushion, to an apron and chef hat, all of which were opportunities to build my skills and make me realize the art of using flat pieces of fabric to craft some dimensional projects. Every project I completed, sparked my ongoing interest in the quilts that Mom and Grandma created.

Grandma suffered from several strokes which left her in the company of strangers, because she no longer recognized her family and acquaintances or knew who her best friend and daughter were. When the strokes erased the memories, her knowledge of crafting was also lost. Her embroidery projects, and numerous quilt squares and patterns waited for someone to finish them. Through the loss of losing Grandma and Grandpa, and the movement of items out of their house into our home when it was sold, they still waited, never being noticed

Mom was always with me, during my childhood and as a young woman, for every doctor's appointment, test, disappointment and achievement. Mom was my best friend and my inspiration along my life journey. The older I became, the more I feared a stroke or dementia entering the picture. When her older brothers were diagnosed with Alzheimer's and Dementia, the genetic factor became a real fear that lingered in the back of my mind. In response, I started with meal planning and cooking with the mindset of maintaining a healthy heart and blood pressure.

Then, despite my best efforts to eliminate the chances of the same stalking strokes stealing Mom from our family, the exact same thing happened to her. Despite visits to doctors, having a proper diet, and plenty of exercise, several small strokes led to her diagnosis of dementia. Suddenly I realized that my Mom and best friend, my mentor and teacher, my caregiver – my everything was going to be erased.

Medications helped her and bought us a wonderful year where her life returned to normal. It provided us a year to say everything we needed to and make memories to keep with us forever. This year also gave me a wonderful opportunity to shift from being the person receiving care to becoming her caregiver.

It was during this year of so many new adjustments, when we were looking for a project to work on together, that we made the discovery – a laundry hamper that had been waiting in the basement for fifteen years. The hamper contained the cardboard patterns and many quilt squares Grandma had sewn to place together for a quilt.

Each quilt square had a story written with pieces of fabric from items in their family life over the past thirty years. Pieces of earth tone square print fabric from shirts Grandma had sewn for Grandpa, and white flowered cotton from dresses for Mom. There were even squares with the blue flowered fabric Grandma had used to sew my Raggedy Ann's dress. Mom and I decided we were going to sew the squares into quilts for our family holiday gifts.

Mom and I made a trip to the store to select a neutral green cotton for the lattice and a neutral for the back that we thought Grandma would approve of using for the lattice. With our supplies we returned home. Due to the arthritis in my fingers and my limiting strength and mobility, using scissors was a challenge for me; so, Dad helped us to cut the numerous long lattice strips. We all worked as a team to secure the squares to the lattice with pins. Then, with Mom's sewing machine threaded and resting on the corner of our dining room table, to enable me to reach it from my wheelchair, we began our journey.

Mom taught me about pinning, seams, ironing and little tricks when creating the quilt. We sat side by side and shared the process of sewing each piece into a larger piece. With every stitch, we were not only growing a quilt with three generations but making memories. The squares and the fabric provided snapshots of lives from the past which triggered memories we were all able to share.

Dad, Mom and I laid the quilt across our entire dining room table to get the batting pinned and ready for sewing. As the quilt was a Queen size, Mom sat next to me and helped to thread the fabric through the machine and ensure no opportunity for bulges or winkles. Once the quilt was sewn together, Dad helped us turn the large quilt inside out.

Then I sewed the space for turning the quilt inside out closed and we began cutting yarn to secure the quilts. Over two days, Mom, Dad and I sat at the table with the quilt spread over our laps as we threaded yarn through and completed securing ties across every few inches of the quilt surface. Once I had given each tied yarn a haircut to ensure a similar length, we admired the quilt.

This was not just any quilt. The pieces of fabrics were from little pieces of memories that linked our family. Grandma started the journey in the past, but the quilt and the love was something that would live on into the future and be an everlasting stitch in the fabric of time.

Author Bio:

No one ever expected Alison Neuman to live past the age of three, let alone become a successful author and performer. Now, an inspirational figure, Neuman has never let the painful disease she suffers with, dermatomyositis, dictate what she can and cannot achieve in her life. An award-winning singer, Neuman has even done dance performances with the iDance and Cripsie Groups in her native Edmonton, Alberta, Canadian hometown. Along the way, she has become a college graduate, earning a degree in creative writing from MacEwen College, despite being told she'd never amount to anything. Searching for Normal is her memoir and anthem to anyone who is suffering through sickness or obstacles that seem too impossible to overcome.

"You can and will achieve life's greatest dreams," Neuman says, "if you take it one step at a time; even if that step is while you navigate via a wheelchair.

Alison's books, *Ice Rose;* and *Searching for Normal: A Memoir* are both available at *www.firesidepubs.com* and at *www.amazon.com.*

The Last Party
by
Sharilynn La May

Students at junior high adored my movie-star-handsome father who taught science. Hence, the popular crowd tolerated me. I wanted more. I longed to mingle with the clique. Maybe a Christmas party would do the trick. I mean, why wouldn't Joann and Sharon and Bonnie and Mary show up? They asked me every day for help with homework. No boys at the party, of course – just the four cheerleaders, the twins across the street and my two best friends. Before breaking for the holidays, I extended eight invitations. Everyone promised to come. Mom helped me plan snacks: deviled eyes, potato chips, tuna fish, ham, and turkey sandwiches cut in triangles. Sweets would be gingerbread men and star-shaped sugar cookies with colored frosting, baked and decorated by my younger sister and me.

Our split-level house had a lower level that we called the family room. A couch and two easy chairs faced our blonde TV and next to it a large mahogany **Zenith** radio and phonograph. Both pieces were old like other odd pieces in the room. Teachers didn't bring home large paychecks in the fifties. Dad had saved to buy Mom her dream house which meant a thrifty Christmas, but wasn't it always – one major gift for me and one for my sister.

Five days before Christmas and two days before the party, Mom and Dad approached me in the living room with a large wrapped package.

"We want to give you your Christmas present early," Dad said.

"Why?" I asked.

Mother answered, "We want you to have it for your party."

My younger sister joined us as I tore open the wrappings and whooped with delight. My own record player! One I could put in my room. But it wasn't just any record player. The blue and cream portable phonograph had Elvis Presley's signature scrawled at the bottom of the black top. My hero!

I hugged myself. I hugged Mom and Dad. I hugged the machine and kissed the signature. Oh yeah – the pop star shook his pelvis in my dreams every night.

My records were stashed in the Zenith. My sister dashed to retrieve them while I unlocked the clasp to reveal a turntable with an arm cradled in a safety hook. Barb brought two Elvis records. Dad plugged in the machine. I placed one 45 rpm on the spindle, turned "ON" and set the needle in the groove. The four of us danced to *Hound Dog.* and *Jailhouse Rock.* – exactly what I pictured my girlfriends and me doing. And wouldn't it impress the trendsetters at school? – the expensive phonograph with my idol's name? This could lead to invitations to their parties.

That night, Mary called.

"My Grandma's decided to visit. I can't come to your party after all."

"Oh," I managed. "I understand."

Mary hung up, too fast it seemed.

Okay, seven plus me would still makes for fun. I guess it was a good excuse. For me, a party would take preference over an old lady who no doubt would stay for a week.

Next morning, one of the twins called, "We're both down with the flu."

Uh, oh. This wasn't looking good. That afternoon, the phone rang again. I recognized Sharon's thin voice.

"My parents want to do last-minute shopping tomorrow night. I have to babysit"

Later that day, Sharon's close friend, Joann, called. By now, I dreaded picking up the receiver. Turned out she and Bonnie couldn't make it either. No excuse offered. On the evening before the party, only two names remained on my list – my best friends, of course.

This time, I made the calls. "No one can come," I told Linda and Susan. "I've decided to cancel."

Did the girls really have good excuses?

I emotionally kicked myself. Of course, they wouldn't waste their time with someone outside their crowd. But I could get over that. What bothered me more? I had stolen Christmas morning from my parents.

You see, seventy-five percent of my pleasure came from watching reactions to gifts I selected for Mom, Dad, and Sister. Throughout the year, I observed what gave them joy. Then I looked for treasures to fit their tastes: a book of poetry for Mom, a fancy lighter for

Dad, a paisley scarf for Sis. The fun of giving far outweighed the fact of getting. I figured this was true of everyone. By giving me an early gift, Mom and Dad couldn't look forward to my excitement that day. I cried about that, not about my party.

"I'm sorry your friends couldn't make it." Mom's arms folded around me. "It's a bad time of year for a party. Everyone has so many unexpected things come up."

"I just feel badly that you gave me my Christmas gift early for nothing,"I sobbed.

"There will still be little surprises under the tree." Mama smiled.

And there were. A red Jonathan Logan dress from Grandma, a wallet from my sister, a diary that locked from Mom and Dad, and some costume jewelry. I put the Elvis record player under the tree anyway and enjoyed watching the pleasure of others as they unwrapped my carefully thought out gifts.

Yet, the memory of those telephone calls still lingers. Did the girls tell the truth? Or did they decide as a group that my party would not be fun. This turn of events affected me more than I expected. I never tried to give another party.

Funny how things stay with you – baggage so trivial in the scheme of life.

Author Bio:

Sharilynn La May is a retired teacher living in Summerfield, Florida, with her couch potato husband and equally lazy cat, Rosie. Her inspirational biographical stories have appeared in *Chicken Soup for the Teacher's Soul, Home Life, Venture Inward,* and *Dolls Remembered.* Three of her play scripts placed in the top five of Writer's Digest Writing Competition. Her recent efforts are in the field of self-publishing. Amazon and Kindle carry *Taking Control: Leaps of Faith,* her husband's success in spite of poverty and lack of education. Just out is her own coming-of-sexual awareness age in *Prince Charming, Where Are You?* or *My Days as a Cherry Girl.*

Christmas Baby, Maybe

Written & Performed
by
Nelson Trout

Sleigh bells ringing
Children singing
Laughing,
Happy as can be
Silver tinsel on the tree.
Still believing
Santa's bringing
Something special
Just for me this year.

And if you'll be my
Christmas Baby, maybe
Sure as Rudolph's nose
Goes down in history,
If you'll be my
Christmas Baby, maybe
Then I'll know Santa
Still believes in me...

Reindeer flying
No children crying
All with presents
Under their tree,
Still believing
Ole' Santa's Bringing
Lots of Christmas cheer
For everyone this year,

So if you'll be
My Christmas Baby, maybe
Sure as Rudolph guides
His sleigh on Christmas Eve,
If you'll be my
Christmas Baby, maybe
Then I'll know Santa
Still believes in me.

If you'll be
My Christmas Baby, maybe
Sure as Mistletoe
Means kisses on Christmas Eve,
If you'll be my
Christmas Baby, maybe,
There'll be no maybes
And I'll know
Santa still believes in me.

Yes, I'll know
Santa still believes in me.

He believes in me!

Nelson Trout is a singer/song writer who lives in New Jersey. Of late, he has turned his creative talents toward prose. His latest book, Raven April, was published by Fireside Publications and can be found on the publisher's website, www.firesidepubs.com as well as on Kindle and Nook. Look for Nelson's Christmas story, *The Singer in the Snow , later* in this anthology.

The Best Gift of All
by
Don Himelstein

Albert sat on the hard bench directly across from his ex- wife Diane, who made it a point not to look at him, or even show any interest at all. The waiting room was crowded with other couples who sat patiently waiting their turn to be called before the Family Court Judge. Albert was sure it was not a pleasant feeling for anyone to be in this court waiting like this, but he tried to make the best it.

The room was dull and colorless, but on the court officer's desk a small Christmas tree sat with the lights blinking; Albert smiled to himself thinking about the holiday that was only a few days away.

The female court officer saw him looking at the tree, and she smiled, but then as if suddenly remembering where she was, her face became a cold mask again. He forced himself to turn away as the door opened and a young couple walked out.

Albert winced as he noticed the mist of tears in the woman's eyes, but the man following her did not look happy either. He watched them as the young man handed a paper to the woman officer at the desk. The couple remained silent but Albert could sense the cold bitterness that separated the two young people.

"If you miss another child support payment Mr. Foley," the woman officer said, "the Court will issue a warrant for your arrest, is that understood?"

"Yes, I understand," he answered in a shaky, weak voice. "I won't miss anymore payments."

"He'd better not," the woman groaned, "I need that money for food to feed my kids."

Albert felt consumed by the anger flaming from her eyes that he guessed had once been young and cheerful. Now they looked cold and hateful, not trusting the world, especially the man standing next to her.

"Alright, you can go now," the officer said.

"Can he stay a moment until I leave?" the young woman asked. "I don't want him near me."

"Okay, you can go first. Mr. Foley, sit down for a few minutes until your wife leaves." Her voice was demanding with authority, and the young man turned and walked to a corner and sat down.

Albert watched the young woman walk quickly out the door but he couldn't bring himself to look at the man; and he noticed that nobody else did either. He glanced at Diane who he knew had watched the whole thing, but she had her head down now and would not look at him. Less than five minutes later a burly male Court Officer called out in a harsh voice…

"Case number 40-16, Docket 12/17, Burk versus Myers, step forward please."

Albert looked across at his wife, who sat up nervously and stared back at him. They both stood up with their court papers in hand. Diane walked ahead of him into the court room. When they got inside, the Officer pointed to where they should stand, and each took a place in front of the Judge's desk. The room felt chilly to Albert. He wished they had the heat up higher, but he also knew that he was nervous, and he could feel a cold chill running down his spine.

He saw Diane looking around with eyes opened wide after she placed her folder on the desk. Then she glanced quickly at him, but her eyes showed a burning anger. He knew that she blamed him for all this conflict. Just as she looked away, the judge walked into the room, and what a surprise! The middle aged woman's short-cropped brown hair was bobbed so close it gave her face a tight-hard expression that made Albert feel uncomfortable.

His throat constricted, and his lips became dry. *This is not going to be good,.* he thought. *I'll leave here an even poorer man than when I came in.*

The judge took her place at the desk in the front of the room. She spoke softly to the Court Officer who showed her the file papers on the case.

"Alright, John," she said in a louder tone. "Are we ready to proceed?"

"We are, Your Honor," John said.

"Is the recorder working properly?"

"It is, Your Honor."

"Then let's get started, we have a lot of cases to process this morning."

The judge turned to Diane and Albert who waited patiently, watching the judge's every motion.

"Court will begin in just a minute," she said.to them.

"And Mr. Myers, please allow your wife to go first.You understand, I'm sure. And I don't want to hear any sudden outburst today, is that understood?"

Albert could sense as much as hear the judge's words, and he knew she meant business. He also knew from speaking with friends of his who had gone through Family Court, that it was a women and children's Court, and that the man was at a disadvantage.

"I understand, your Honor," he said, softly.

She gave him a hard, cold look.

"Fine, now that we understand each other we can proceed."

She nodded to the Court Officer, who turned on the recorder.

"Docket 12/17, case 40 -16, child support

in the manner of two minor children, ages seven and nine. Now, Ms Burk have you received your

Court ordered support for the months of September through November?"

"I have not, Your Honor," Diane called out in a high, pitched voice.

The judge turned with heavy, penetrating eyes on Albert.

"Mr. Myers, can you explain to the court why you have not made Court ordered payment of due child support arrears?'

"I was out of work, Your Honor," Albert answered, his voice scratchy and sad. "I had no means of support or income to make payment."

"What do you do for a living, Mr. Myers?"

"I was salesman, Your Honor, in stationary; the company went out of business three months ago."

"How long did you work for that company, Mr. Myers?"

"Six and a half years, Your Honor," he answered. "It was a good company, but the economy slowed down, and business began to drop off. They had to lay off people, and finally it closed down."

"That's unfortunate, Mr. Myers," she said, after a moment, but it's your obligation to support your family."

After a quick glance at the papers on her desk, she looked up at his wife.

"Ms. Burk, your last child support payment came in August, is that correct?"

"It is Your Honor," Diane called out in a teary voice. "I haven't received a dime in support since then; I need rent money, food for the children, very little is coming in."

"Alright, Ms. Burk, we understand," the judge said in a soothing voice. Shifting a bit to her right, she focused on John and asked, "Now, Mr. Myers, has your financial situation changed in recent weeks?"

"Yes, Your Honor, I started working for a delivery service driving a truck."

"When did you begin working for this company, Mr. Myers?"

"About three weeks ago, Your Honor," Albert said, his voice stained with nervousness.

"Have you received a paycheck with your new employment?"

"I got my first paycheck last week."

"How much was it for, Mr. Myers?"

"It was for five hundred and fifty two dollars, Your Honor."

"Now Mr. Myers, according to court records your child support is in the amount of four hundred and fifty dollars per month, which means you owe thirteen hundred and fifty dollars in back support payments. Is that correct?"

Albert sighed deeply.

"It is, Your Honor."

"Do you have the back support arrears payment in that amount at this time, Mr. Myers?"

"I do not, Your Honor, all I can do is give you part of my paycheck now, and as my situation improves try to make up the rest as soon as I can."

"Where are you currently living, Mr. Myers?" the judge asked.

"I'm staying with my mother for the time being."

"I see," the judge said.

She glanced at Diane who stood nervously waiting for her turn to speak.

"Now, Ms. Burk, I believe your ex-husband is trying to make amends with past child support. What if he gave you a partial payment out of his last paycheck of four hundred and fifty dollars and made up the rest in arrears payments to catch up. Does that seem fair?"

Albert crumbled under the rush of resentment burning in Diane's eyes. He knew she didn't want only the back support. She wanted him in jail – and to have no contact with his daughters. Not now – not ever.

"No! Your Honor. I need that money now. Today! And I don't think he should get off that easy."

"But he has tried, Ms. Burk, to make restitution on back child support payments. Mr. Myers was out of work. He should have contacted us immediately, but he is employed again, so hopefully, he can make up the arrears, and take care of his obligations."

Albert saw the killer look in Diane's eyes. and he knew at once what was going to happen.

"Your Honor, I don't want my ex husband to see the children during the Christmas holiday. All he does is upset them, and I don't think he should have any contact with them right now."

The judge raised her hand as if to stop her from speaking.

"Ms. Burk, do you think that is fair not to allow your ex-husband to see his children during the Christmas holiday?"

Diane tightened her face, and Albert could see her eyes changing to a darker color.

"Yes, I do! He didn't pay his child support then why should he have the right to see his children during the holiday?"

"Mr. Myers," the judge said to him. "Is there anything you would like to say?"

Albert felt the burning in his throat, but then he steadied himself, knowing he could not let himself get angry. He also knew that it would break his heart not to see his kids on Christmas, to be with them, to hold them, hug them, and watch their faces when they opened their gifts. With all the strength he had left to fight; he pulled himself together for this emotional battle.

"Your Honor, my kids mean everything in the world to me; and not to see them at Christmas time would be a hardship that I would find almost impossible to live with. I'm trying all I can to be a good father, to support my family in the best way that I can. Sometimes it's been hard, and life doesn't always work out, but you keep right on trying, not giving up. I know I haven't always been the best father in the world, but I love my children with all my heart, and I would never hurt them."

"Mr. Myers," the judge cut in, "that's all well and good, but you are in arrears of support payments, and the Court must take that into consideration."

"Your Honor," Albert replied, his voice cracking with the pain in his throat. "If I have too I'll work another job, I'll go without – that I promise. But please, don't keep me away from my kids – not ever, but certainly not during the Christmas Holiday. I was away for two years in the army and missed those Christmas times with my family. I don't want to do that again, not with my children."

"Please, Your Honor."

The judge actually turned away to stare at the Court Officer who stood quietly near her side.

Albert thought she looked uncomfortable, as if she didn't quite know what to do, and was asking the Court Officer for help. But then she turned back and gave each of then a hard, determined look.

"This court must make a decision as to what is best for the minor children," the judge said. "With due respect to both parties in question, the court feels that Ms. Burk has just cause to want full arrears child support payment, and understands the need to keep Mr. Myers from allowing him any contact with his minor children.

"However, the court also feels that Mr. Myers is making every effort to bring his arrears in order, and at this time he should be allowed to visit with his minor children during this holiday season. So the court will allow visitation during the Christmas holiday. Payment in arrears of four hundred and fifty dollars will start today. Thank you both.

"Court is dismissed."

The big court officer moved toward the door and opened it.

"Alright, if you'll please step outside the judge will have your Court Order in a few minutes."

Albert followed his ex-wife out the door and into the quiet room full of couples waiting their turn to go before the judge. He felt his body shaking with relief, and he immediately knew he had won the very best gift of all – he would see his children at Christmas, and nothing else really mattered at that moment.

Author Bio

Donald Himelstein served two years in the United States Army as a medical corpsman stationed in Germany. After his discharge, he received his AAS degree from Kingsborough Community college and his BA degree from Richmond College, now College of Staten Island. He retired some years ago after more than 33 years of service with the New York State Office of Disability as an Analyst. His first novel, *ABOVE HONOR: Rachel's Story*, was published in 2010 by Fireside Publications and is still available on the publisher's website, www.firesidepubs.com and on Amazon.com/kindle.

Tootsie's Christmas
by
R.M. Prioleau

December, 1956

Today was one of the most fun days of the year. With only seven days till Christmas, Mama let me come with her to Woolworth's that morning, so she could do her usual shopping. But I always loved coming here during the holidays, because I knew the store would be decked out in Christmas stuff everywhere. As Mama and I crossed Fordham Road, I could already see through the fancy glass doors to the big Christmas tree in the middle of the store, all covered in lights and garland. I wished we had a tree that big too, but we'd never be able to fit it in our apartment.

Once we were inside the store, Mama let go of my hand and looked at me sternly.

"Behave, Rita. Stay in the toy section."

I grinned up at her as she removed my mittens, loosened my scarf, and unbuttoned my wool coat. I certainly had no interest in going anywhere else in the store, anyway.

"I will, Mama."

I sped off toward the toy section as fast as my bright red snow boots could take me. I was in heaven. Toys were everywhere. Mountains and mountains of toys! Other kids wandered around, some tugging their parents along. It was so close to Christmas, and I still hadn't written a letter to Santa yet. I really wanted a puppy, but Mama said Santa told her that pets weren't allowed in the building, so I'd have to think of something else.

I passed by a fancy tea set display and thought about my friend, Susan, who'd always invite me, Bonnie, and Shirley over for tea parties.

A Dick Tracy jigsaw puzzle caught my eye, and I wandered over to the display where other kids and their parents gathered. I bet Bonnie already put this on her list for Santa already. She loved puzzles, and *really* loved Dick Tracy – like me. She had been good this year, so I would bet Santa would get it for her, and then I could go over to her house and play with it, too.

I wandered through the seemingly endless aisles of toys and stopped at the doll section, where a display of the new Pretty Posies sat. I didn't play with dolls as much as Shirley. She had tons of them. But I knew she didn't have a Pretty Posie yet. No doubt, already she wrote to Santa about that.

Next to the dolls were the stuffed animals of all shapes and sizes. But there was one that really caught my eye…

I picked up a brown stuffed dachshund, my favorite kind of dog because they look like my favorite kind of candy: Tootsie Rolls. This dachshund wore a red and white collar with "Tootsie Roll" written on it. Along the back of the dog was a small zipper. I carefully unzipped it, revealing a hidden pocket.

I grinned.

Perfect!

I could probably fit a dozen Midgee Tootsie Rolls in there. *Midgee. That's what I'll call her.*

Looked like I found the perfect present to tell Santa about.

"Ready to go?" Mama called from behind me. I jumped, not realizing she was done with her shopping already.

"Mama, I think I know what I want Santa to get me," I said.

She smiled softly. "What is it?"

"Well, since I can't get a real pet, how about…" I showed her the dachshund, and she raised her eyebrows.

"A stuffed dog?"

"It's not any dog, Mama!" I showed her the hidden zipper and told her my plans for stashing Tootsie Rolls.

Mama laughed. "Okay, I don't see why Santa couldn't get you that. It's not technically a *real* pet, after all. I guess you'll have to write that letter, eh?"

I nodded firmly and set the stuffed animal back in its place. "You bet I will!"

Later that day, Bonnie, Shirley, and Susan came over to look at holiday catalogs. Bonnie and I were scouring the toys in the JC Penney one, while Shirley and Susan ogled at the dolls and princess-looking dresses in the Sears one. I told my friends about the stuffed dachshund I wanted, and Bonnie agreed to help me find it in one of the catalogs to cut out. It wasn't long before we found it, along with other neat toys that

I knew would make my list even longer. But Mama said that if I made my list too long, then Santa would think I was being greedy, and greedy kids were bad. So, I decided to play it safe and ask for one thing. I cut out the picture from the catalog and pasted it on a piece of white construction paper. I wrote a quick letter to Santa in crayon, alternating each word in red and brown, so it would remind him of Tootsie Rolls. I even signed my name and drew a little Tootsie Roll at the bottom. Afterward, I folded the letter neatly.

"Wanna play Chutes and Ladders?" Susan asked, closing the catalog.

I shook my head. "Maybe later. I gotta go to the post office and mail this to Santa."

"We'll go with you, Tootsie," Bonnie said.

On our way out, I asked Daddy for an envelope. I also asked him for a stamp, but Daddy said US stamps didn't work in the North Pole, and I'd have to draw a special stamp for Santa. I drew a stamp with a Tootsie Roll on it, so Santa would know this letter came from me. I addressed the envelope, stuffed the letter inside, then sealed it—yuck.

Outside, we found some of the neighborhood kids building snow forts and having snowball fights.

Roy poked his head from one of the finished forts and smirked at us. "Intruders! Prepared to be pulverized!"

My friends and I looked toward the fort, and more of Roy's friends appeared. They each held a snowball in their mittened hands.

"Explain yourself, intruders," Charlie said, "and we just might let you live."

I fumed. I hated Roy and his friends. They were always so mean to us. Well, sometimes Roy did nice things for me, but most of the time he didn't. Boys were so weird.

"We're mailing a letter to Santa," Susan said, her hands on her hips.

The boys laughed. "What'd you ask for this time?" Roy said. "Another dolly-wolly?"

"We're not telling you," I snapped.

"Hmph. Well *I'm* gonna get a bunch of new scale-model cars and trucks. Since Santa's a boy, he knows what cool toys are."

My friends and I rolled our eyes.

The boys went back to hiding in their fort, leaving us alone, thankfully. We continued to the post office.

"Him and his dumb cars," I muttered. "I hope they all get a stocking full of coal for picking on us like that."

"You shouldn't say that," Bonnie said. "My daddy said if you wish bad things on people then that makes you bad, too."

I grimaced. Golly, I didn't think about it like that. I hoped Santa didn't hear it, either.

We arrived at the post office two blocks later, and Mr. Russo, the courier, was there sorting mail. On top of the counter was a big gift-wrapped box with a little slot on the top. A sign that said "Letters to Santa" sat beside the box. This was the box that all the kids used to send their letters.

As I slid my letter through the slot, Mr. Russo looked up at us and smiled. "Well, hello, girls. All ready for Christmas this year?"

"You bet!" we all said together.

"Great," he said. "We'll be delivering this next batch of mail to the North Pole tomorrow. But, ah...we have so many letters this year. We might need some help. Think you can ask your parents to come by tomorrow and help us deliver the mail to Santa?"

My eyes widened, and I gaped. "I sure will!" I said.

"Us too!" my friends said.

Wow, Mama and Daddy would get to deliver mail to the North Pole. They'd get to see Santa! How great was that?

When we returned to our street, the boys had finished their forts, and some girls were making snow angels while the rest were building a snowman. My friends and I ignored the boys and joined the snowman-making girls as they rolled around the piece that would be the head.

"Let's make her a princess," one of the girls said. "I have a tiara from my birthday party."

As I gathered more snow, I was suddenly struck hard from behind. Boys' laughter followed.

I glared over my shoulder at Roy and his friends in their fort, building an arsenal of snowballs. I noticed my bottom was covered in snow. Those darned boys! They threw a snowball at me!

I abandoned the snowman and started gathering snow in my hand for nice big snowball to launch right back at them. "You asked for it!" I said then aimed for Roy, who watched me, amused.

"Ha ha! You can't hit us!" Roy teased.

Gritting my teeth, I launched the snowball as hard as I could toward the boys. They hid back in their fort, and the ball bounced off a wall and took a small chunk of snow with it.

Shirley, Bonnie, Susan, and the rest of the girls stopped their work and came to my rescue.

"C'mon! Let's teach those boys a lesson!" Susan yelled, making a good-sized snowball.

"Snowball fight!" Bonnie yelled.

It was boys against girls as snowballs flew everywhere. We'd ended up destroying half of their fort, and hitting a few of the boys, but all the girls got hit at least once – even Bonnie, who was probably the only one of us who was really good at snowball fights. The fight lasted a while and soon we were all exhausted, our arms hurting like crazy. But it was fun, and we all laughed – the boys, too.

As we all lay in the snow, Mrs. Robinson, the candy store owner's wife, who lived two floors above me, came outside the building to stand on the stoop holding a tray of steaming paper cups.

"Any of you children want some hot chocolate?" she asked.

We all sprang up from the snowy ground and raced over to the woman, surrounding her in a tight circle.

"Me! Me!" we all shouted, raising our hands.

She chuckled and began passing out the cups, one by one. "Okay, okay. There's plenty for everyone."

She handed me a steaming-hot cup, and my mittened hands allowed me to hold it. When all the kids were served, she went back inside. The kids sat around, enjoying their hot chocolate, which had tiny marshmallows floating around it.

Well, all of them had marshmallows except for mine.

I frowned. I loved marshmallows in hot chocolate. There was something about marshmallows that made it taste better. Maybe mine melted or something. Or maybe Mrs. Robinson forgot to put some in mine.

I sat on one of the steps of the stoop and stared at the swirling chocolate in my cup. Roy sat next to me. The boys and girls were currently doing a truce while we enjoyed our chocolate.

"What are you frownin' about now, Tootsie?" Roy asked, scrunching his brow.

I looked at him and pouted, then stared back at my cup.

"Everyone else has marshmallows but me," I replied.

He leaned over to get a peek at my cup.

"Huh."

He looked in his cup, then at mine again, twisting his lips as though unsure of himself, plucked a marshmallow from his cup, then put it in mine.

"There."

I blinked in surprise then stared at the lone marshmallow floating in my cup, like a paper boat lost at sea. I smiled at Roy, though I didn't mean to. But sometimes he did nice things for me, and I couldn't help it.

"Gee whiz, thanks, Roy."

He rolled his eyes and scooted a few inches away from me.

"Yeah, yeah."

I took a nice long sip of chocolate, savoring the hint of the marshmallowy taste. I hoped Santa got Roy all the cars and trucks he wanted.

On Christmas morning, I sprung out of bed and rushed to the living room, where presents of all shapes and sizes sat under the big aluminum tree. I found the presents for me and noticed they were all addressed to "Rita" instead of "Tootsie." Maybe Santa forgot my nickname. He was pretty busy having to remember all the kids' names, so I guess that was okay.

I quickly unwrapped the present, hoping Midgee would be inside.

To my dismay, it was just a pair of pink jumpers. Pink? Ugh! I hated pink!

As I reached for another present, Mama came into the living room wearing her flowery robe.

"Rita, you need to eat breakfast first before you open any more presents," she said.

I pouted.

"But Mama, I want to see if Santa got me Midgee."

She eyed me sternly. "No buts. Now go eat breakfast." She pointed to the kitchen.

My face fell, and I reluctantly dragged myself out of the living room, to the kitchen, where Daddy sat at his usual spot at the table in his robe, reading his paper.

He reached for his coffee and looked to me curiously.

"Why the long face on Christmas?"

I slid into my chair and eyed the empty bowl, cereal box, and bottle of milk placed before me.

"I wanna open my presents."

Daddy chuckled, then sipped his coffee before sticking his face in front of the paper.

"Well hurry and eat some breakfast, and you can open all the presents you want."

I poured some cereal, and the prize inadvertently fell out into my Grape-Nuts Flakes. An aluminum scale-model semitruck, as advertised on the box. I set the truck aside and filled my bowl with milk.

Daddy peered from behind his paper.

"You found the prize?"

I nodded, and slowly munched on my cereal.

"Yeah, just a truck." I wished Mama could've gotten the cereals with the airplanes or puzzles inside, instead. Oh well. Maybe one of the boys would want it.

I wolfed down the rest of my breakfast then returned to the living room to finish opening my presents. I ended up getting more clothes – some nicer than my ugly pink one – a farm playset, and a jump rope. But no Midgee. I sighed and took my unwrapped presents to my room. I still liked the presents I got, and I planned on playing with them a lot, but I just wished I could've gotten Midgee. Afterward, I washed up, got dressed and grabbed the jump rope, then headed to the door. I bet Santa got the other kids what they wanted. I'd just have fun playing with them today.

"Wait, Rita," Daddy called as I was about to leave.

I turned and noticed him knelt before the tree, reaching for a present in the very back. It was definitely well hidden, and anyone could've easily missed it. The box was small and long and wrapped in paper that had pictures of Santa on it.

"Looks like you missed this one." Daddy said, handing it to me.

I dropped the rope to grab the box, which was addressed to "Tootsie." My eyes lit up. *He remembered my name!*

"It's from Santa!" I exclaimed.

"Well, aren't you going to open it?"

I ripped open the present then pulled out the stuffed dachshund.

"It's Midgee!"

I hugged and cuddled her, but I felt something odd. I examined her then unzipped the top. Inside were dozens of Midgee Tootsie Rolls. My eyes widened, and I gaped. "Wow! So many!"

Daddy smiled and winked.

"Looks like Santa didn't forget, eh?"

"I can't wait to show my friends!" I said, rushing out the door.

There were kids already outside playing in the snow and showing off their new presents. I found my friends, who all got what they wanted for Christmas, too.

"I'll invite you all for tea tomorrow then we can use my brand new tea set," Susan said.

"Can Posie come, too?" Shirley asked.

"Of course!"

I spotted Roy sitting with his friends, while they played with their new toys. He didn't say much and looked a little sad. I left my friends for a while and went over to Roy to show him Midgee.

"Hey, Roy, look what Santa got me." I said, smiling.

Roy took one look at Midgee and sneered.

"What's it to you, Tootsie? It's just a dumb dog."

My smile fell.

"It's an awesome dog that guards all my Tootsie Rolls!"

"Yeah, well you have fun with that." He idly picked up a toy airplane and flicked at the propeller bitterly.

"What's wrong?" I asked.

"All Santa got me were clothes. I asked my mom and dad why Santa didn't answer my letter, and they said they talked to Santa, and he told them that I already had lots of cars and trucks and wouldn't have room for any more. So he got me clothes – lots of ugly clothes."

I frowned. "Yeah, he got me ugly clothes, too. I can't believe he thinks I like pink!"

"Pink is a girly color, that's why. Anyway, you still got your stuffed dog – you still got what you wanted, so what does it matter to you?"

"You shouldn't be sad on Christmas..." I paused and suddenly thought up an idea. *Of course!* I turned back to Roy.

"Stay right here. I'll be right back.

I rushed bak to my apartment, to the kitchen and grabbed the toy truck. I returned to Roy with it.

"It's not much, but Merry Christmas, Roy," I said, handing it to him.

Roy blinked and took the truck.

"Wow, you got the aluminum version! I've been trying to get this version for a long time!" He looked up at me. "You're really giving this to me?"

I nodded once. "You bet. Let's build a tunnel in the snow for it."

He grinned. "Sounds like fun."

We played with the truck all day. I had more fun with Roy than I did the other kids. And most of all, Roy was really happy. Maybe Santa *did* answer his letter after all.

Author Bio:

R.M Prioleau

R.M. Prioleau is a game developer and artist by day; and a dangerous writer by night. Since childhood, she's continued exploring new methods of expanding her skills and creativity as she delves into the realm of literary abandon. R.M. can often be seen lurking about many great writing communities like NaNoWriMo. R.M. is the author of the epic fantasy series, "The Pyromancer Trilogy", and "The Necromancer's Apprentice", her debut gothic fantasy novella, which was awarded first place in the 2013 Royal Palm Literary Awards. She has also written numerous short stories, one of which won first place in the 2014 Royal Palm Literary Awards.

The Singer in the Snow
by
Nelson Trout

Edna roused up while lying face down in the snow. She couldn't be sure just how long she had been there. The sky overhead was dark, but she could see store lights twinkling along the top of the new fallen snowflakes.

Less than ten feet lay between Edna and the edge of darkness. People were walking in and out of the last store in the strip-mall, a small grocery shop where Edna had just purchased half a dozen apples and a small bunch of bananas. They walked near, *oh* so near to where the light ended; cut off by the corner of the building.

Edna lay blended into the darkness of the parking lot. She tried to wave a hand; she tried to scream and draw attention to her dreadful situation until her neck muscles became weak, and her face would fall mercilessly back into the snow – snow which was falling hard and fast now. A smile crossed her near-frozen face at the thought of having a white Christmas, as she herself was quickly being covered in the relentless, unexpected snow storm.

It's sad to be alone on Christmas Eve, much worse to be stranded, knowing that no one will be looking for you. Thoughts raced across her sixty-five year old mind – good thoughts – scary thoughts – realistic thoughts; she may actually die here tonight in this strip-mall parking lot and meet the Lord on Christmas Eve.

Edna cried silently, then tried to sing "Silent Night", but only the weak whisper of a lonely, and now desperate woman could be heard, and only heard by the singer herself, *the singer in the snow*. She began to drift off to sleep.

Edna was losing her battle with Multiple Sclerosis. Her body was failing, yet her mind was still razor sharp. She had fought so hard these past eighteen years, and tonight the disease was on its way toward claiming victory – victory over a fighter with the heart of a lion, a battle-hardened champion finally defeated. Asleep now, Edna had no choice but to depend on pleasant dreams, praying that those *not so pleasant dreams* would not haunt her tonight – not on Christmas Eve.

Edna dreamed of Christmases-past – ones she had long ago celebrated with her mother, father and sister Eileen as a little girl before daddy died and mother re-married. Everything seemed different after that. She smiled unconsciously thinking of the year Santa left her and Eileen a cuddly puppy which beame the centerpiece of love in their lives for the next fourteen years. She drifted into the long ago Christmas morning that she and her sister got their first bicycles. Asleep now, Edna's dreams turned to *the* nightmare – the same nightmare that always seemed to invade her peaceful slumber, and wake her in a chilling tremble.

Drifting In and out of sleep in the parking lot, her voice begins to carry a bit louder on the cold December breeze as Edna screams.

"No, no, please don't take my baby…he is mine!"

Her mother talks softly, but with an overshadowing tone of evil.

"Now Edna, we talked about this. We made a deal. The Hudsons are waiting downstairs for their baby. They will give little Richard a good…"

Edna screams.

"Richard? I already named my baby boy Kevin. Kevin is his name – my little Kevin!"

Edna pulls the baby even closer and tighter, enveloping him, her precious little treasure from God, firmly against her body for the last time. Crying hysterically, her mother talks over her and demands the baby, now!

Edna's step-father dashes into Edna's bedroom, and out muscles little *Richard* out of Edna's arms.

"The Hudsons are getting irritated and are threatening to pull the offer if the baby isn't downstairs in five minutes. Mrs. Hudson is crying. Edna, say good-bye. This is what is best for the baby. The Hudsons will give the child a good home. You know we can't afford to keep a baby; besides, you're not married and that bastard *Billy* you thought you loved is gone and never coming back, and you know it Edna".

The last thing Edna saw on her three day-old *Kevin* was the heart-shaped birthmark on his inner left forearm. She *adored* that perfect and quite prominent imperfection. She heard the celebration downstairs when the Hudsons saw her baby; she also knew that his new parents had handed over ten thousand dollars in cash to buy Edna's beautiful little boy. That devious plan had been suggested the very day Edna announced to her parents that she was pregnant. But for nine months, she was able to put that wicked *impossibility* out of her mind.

Edna had just turned twenty and should be able to make her own decisions, but she was sickly as a child, even having to attend her last year of High School at home. Shortly after her nineteenth birthday, Edna was swept off her feet by a handsome young man. Following her doctor's suggestion that she get more fresh air several times a week, Edna was taking a short walk to the near-by park. She found a comfortable bench in a shady spot near the water and sat down to read.

A young man passing by asked if he might sit down on the bench to rest a bit. She agreed, and they soon struck up a conversation. They both enjoyed each other's company; Edna was especially flattered that such a nice guy would take an interest in her.

Within a month, they were dating; eventually this meant going to Billy's apartment to have sex. As happens in many short-term relationships, as soon as Billy found out about the pregnancy, he vanished. Billy and a male room-mate moved two counties away, both finding good jobs and saving up their money. Billy never came back or told anyone, even his family how he could be contacted. It was rumored Billy had moved to California, but no one knew for sure where the father of Edna's baby was living at that time..

"Hey Dad, do you think Santa got my letter?"

Richard laughed, "I think he got it, buddy. We addressed it to the North Pole didn't we?"

"Yep, we sure did". Kevin replied excitedly.

"That doesn't mean you'll *get* everything on your list, but Santa will do his best".

"Dad, I *really* hope I get a puppy, I've been praying every single night. I don't really care about getting anything else this Christmas, except a new baseball glove."

Richard laughs again and ruffles young Kevin's hair.

"Well, we better get home so you and mom and I are asleep when Santa arrives. He'll need Rudolph tonight with all of this snow."

"Oh yeah, he'll need Rudolph for sure tonight, Dad!" Kevin, smiling and looking up into the sky agrees.

Then Kevin abruptly stops walking.

"Dad, do you hear that? Listen. I think I hear someone crying or something". Father and son both stop to listen. Edna was still talking in her sleep, but louder now than when she was still awake.

(This strange but true phenomenon, which doctors cannot fully understand, just may have helped save Edna's life tonight)

"Yeah buddy, I hear it now, too. It's coming from next to the little grocery store. I know you're getting to be a big boy now, but hold my hand; it's dark on that side of the building".

Kevin saw Edna first.

"Dad look, there's somebody over there!"

Edna had stopped reliving her nightmare out loud and lay still and quiet in the pristine falling snow.

Running to Edna, Richard gently held her fragile wrist as he checked her pulse and began lightly brushing the snow away from her face.

"Thank God" he said. "She's still alive.

Kevin, wanting to help, started talking into Edna's ear.

"Mam, ma m, it's alright- you're gonna be alright". Kevin helped his father try and get the woman to a seated position, thinking it might help bring her back into consciousness.

"Dad, is she going be alright?" Kevin asked. Although worried and a little scared, he didn't want to let his father know.

"Listen Kevin," Richard answers, "stay right here with her, and keep talking to her. We've got to get her warm. I'm running over to get the car. You'll be able to see me the whole way. Don't let her lay back down. If you keep talking to her, she might wake up".

"Okay Dad, I've got her". Richard took off for the car, running nearly as fast as he did on the football field back in his high school days.

Edna opened her eyes with snowflakes still resting on her long eyelashes, startling Kevin. "God bless you young man," she said. "If you will help me to my feet, I think I can make it home."

"Where's your car"? Kevin asks her.

Edna, trying but failing to push herself all the way up to her feet, sat back down. "I don't have a car. I only live two blocks away."

She pointed down the street – right around that corner, two blocks down. I'll make it my little hero, if I can just get to my feet. Oh my, and would you *please* be so kind as to help me find my cane? It has to be…"

"I found it, Kevin announced proudly. "I found your cane. It was right next to you almost covered up in the snow. I found a grocery bag too, with apples and bananas."

Smiling broadly, she reached out toward Kevin for the cane. "Oh, the apples and bananas are mine, too. Thank you again my little hero."

Pulling his new Ford Fusion up to the touching scene, Richard wiped a tear from his eye as he watched his young son helping an elderly woman on Christmas Eve- He replaced his cell phone in the glove compartment after calling 911 and left his headlights on, illuminating the Christmas miracle; it almost seemed like a Hollywood movie.

Please God, he thinks, *never let me forget this moment in time.*

Richard finally gets out of his car and briskly walks the few steps over to Edna and Kevin. He stoops down to speak with the woman face to face. He was still afraid she might die before the ambulance arrived.

"May I ask your name, young lady; and how you are feeling right now"?

Edna was still sitting in the snow with little Kevin's arm around her shoulders.

"My name is Edna, she said, and please let me thank you and my little hero here. He even bagged up my apples and bananas. I'm feeling much better now. I better be on my way."

"Yeah, they were all over Dad – and I found every one and put them back in the bag for Miss Edna."

"I'm very proud of you Kevin."

"Did you just call him Kevin?"

She looked at her little hero and asked, "Is your name Kevin?"

"Yes Mam, but you can call me Kevie like my Mom does."

Richard insisted she sit in the car for a while.

"The heat is on Edna. Let's go get you warmed up, okay?"

After thinking about it for a few seconds she acquiesced.

"Yes, I think I would like that, I *am* feeling cold, especially my hands. Bless you".

Between Edna's determination and Richard and Kevin's assistance, they escorted her into the front passenger's seat of Richard's new car. Edna was impressed. "It feels like we're in the cockpit of a jet plane," she said.

Richard laughed.

"Well, I guess that means you like my new car. Thank you Edna."

The lights were very visible, and the sirens were deafening to their ears. "Well, now you'll be in good hands, here comes the ambulance".

"Ambulance for what – for whom?" Edna wanted to know.

"For you Edna, I called them and they…"

"Well, please, please, what is your name?"

"Richard."

"Well Richard, *please* call them again, right now and tell them I'm fine and I do not need to go to the hospital. Please Richard, I'm begging you; I'm *fine* now that I'm warm, honestly. I am terrified of hospitals- terrified!"

"Dad, Miss Edna only lives two blocks away. Why can't we just take her home? Miss Edna, is it alright if my Dad and me take you home?"

"Yes, yes, please take me home. I'm begging you not to let the ambulance take me. Please, anything but that!"

Richard turned the dome light on in the car and took a discerning look at Edna. He had to admit to himself that she did look fairly well. He didn't have the heart to let the ambulance take her to the hospital, especially on Christmas Eve. But he was also thinking prudently. If he was to turn away the ambulance and something happened to Edna at home all alone, he may be held responsible. He decided to offer Edna a deal.

"Okay Edna, I'll tell the ambulance guys that it was a false alarm, we are very sorry, Merry Christmas, blah, blah blah. But, if I do that, you have to spend tonight at our house. I will *not* allow you to go home alone. So which is it, us or them? Edna, you have to tell me so I know; here they are, now.

Edna began to cry; barely audible; then she looked at Richard and said, "You."

"Deal" says Richard, and gets out of the car to meet the ambulance crew as they pulled up. The driver puts the window down, and stuck his head out.

"What's the problem? We were told there was a person lying in the snow possibly near death." Thank *God*, Richard *did* know one of the ambulance crew; they had played football together in high school. He was in the passenger's seat, the snow was flying into the ambulance from the driver's open window. The driver was getting slightly perturbed. Richard talks across him. He was about ready to lie.

"Hi Willie, how ya doin?' Man, do you remember that game we played in weather like this".

"Hey Richard, darn right I remember *that* game," Willie replied. we both scored a touchdown." They both laughed at the great memory and Willie said, "So what's up here buddy? I don't see a body in the snow.".

Richard squints his eyes from the snow.

"No, she's a relative of mine, and she's in the car. She's spending Christmas with us. Look, she wondered away for a moment there and I saw her lying on the ground. I panicked and called you guys. I'm really sorry; hey look, Merry Christmas you guys, and it's so great to see you Willie".

Willie replies, "You too Richie, it's been too long – drive careful, buddy". And off the vehicle with all the lights and sirens into the snowy night before Christmas, Richard had been successful. Now Edna was his responsibility for Christmas Eve and Christmas.

"Buckle up Kevin, we're heading home. Here Edna, let me help you get your seat belt on".

"Thank you", Edna replied. Her fingers were still stiff from the cold.

Richard strapped his own seat-belt on. Kevin and Edna had been talking about something. Kevin was probably telling her how much he wanted a puppy. "Edna, how are you dear, is there anything you need from home before you enjoy a Hudson Christmas Eve and Christmas? We're having milk and cookies tonight and Turkey tomorrow. I cook the best turkey in the State of Pennsylvania –right Kevin?"

"Right, Dad". Then Kevin asked from the backseat, Miss Edna, can I sit next to you at dinner tomorrow? Would that be okay, dad"?

"Sure buddy, if it's alright with Edna."

"Thanks Dad. You know Miss Edna, I'm glad we found you. We never have any guests at Christmas because our relatives all live so far away and my mom's parents both died."

Richard broke in, "Edna, we have a nice guest room for you with your own bathroom and a closet full of clothes that are just about your size. How does a nice hot bath sound to you?

Edna smiled.

"Actually, she said, "it sounds fabulous. May I please stop home to feed my cat? He'll be alone for Christmas, but he doesn't care," she laughed. "All Gunther does is sleep anyway. Oh yes, and eat! I'll grab some clothes too. You really don't know how much I appreciate you saving me from that ambulance. And absolutely, I would be honored to sit next to you for Christmas dinner Kevin; after all, you are my hero."

"Edna," Richard added, "you really are about the same size as Linda, my wife. I'm sure she has a lot of clothes that would look great on you."

"Thank you Richard." They pulled up in front of Edna's little house. It was kind of cute. Richard thought it looked like a gingerbread house all covered in snow. Edna promises, "I'll only be a moment. Kevin, would you like to come in and meet Gunther?"

"Yeah, Dad, can I go in and meet the cat?"

"Sure buddy, and hold on to Edna's arm. Make sure she doesn't slip in the snow."

Edna and Kevin were only in the house for about fifteen minutes. Edna went into her tiny bedroom and packed a small bag. Kevin sat on the well-worn sofa with Gunther on his lap. When Edna was done packing and walked back into the living room, she exclaimed with a laugh, "My goodness, Gunther is not usually that friendly with new people. He likes you Kevin. You must be special. Come along young man, let's not keep your father waiting. You are welcome to come and visit Gunther anytime you'd like." Miss Edna, do you think I'll get a puppy for Christmas"?

"Well, have you been a good boy all year long?"

"Yep!"

"Well then, there's a good chance you'll *get* that puppy. We'll find out tomorrow morning. No matter what, I have a strange but happy feeling that tomorrow is going to be a once-in-a-lifetime Christmas." She smiles. "Let's go Kevin." Edna then pets Gunther and says, "Mommy loves you," before they leave the house.

Richard called Linda on his cell phone. "Honey, we'll be home in less than five minutes. Be prepared for a houseguest."

Linda, surprised, replies "A what?"

Richard, as he smiles at Edna, asks Linda to "Please get the guest room ready? Lay one of your warm, furry robes across the bed. See you in a few. Love you."

"Love you too." Richard thought that Linda sounded confused. But Linda was one of the most caring people Richard had ever met. She would love Edna, and Edna would feel the same about Linda. Richard was comfortably certain of that.

The black Ford Fusion pulled into the driveway, and the three gleeful passengers waited for the garage door to automatically open when Edna remarks, "this is so exiting!" Richard drove carefully into the garage.

"Okay, everybody out. Let's go in and see Mom. Linda will adore you Edna. She is a wonderful person". Right, Kevin?"

He looks at Edna and smiles.

"Yeah, my Mom is pretty cool."

Linda opened the door that opens into the kitchen of the family's large, expensive house. She and Richard kiss. Kevin hurries into the great-room to see the beautiful Christmas tree the family of three had beautifully decorated earlier in the day.

"Honey, this is Edna, our Christmas guest. Don't forget to set another place at the table tomorrow."

Linda, smiling brightly welcomes Edna into her home with a hug.

"Merry Christmas, Edna! I am *so* happy to meet you, and absolutely thrilled to have you here as our Christmas guest."

Edna, holding back tears of pure joy hugs Linda back.

"I'm so happy to be here. Richard was right when he told me how nice and kind you are, Linda. I didn't bring a lot with me. I did bring…"

Linda kindly interrupts, "Edna, why don't you take a hot bath and warm your bones. I understand you spent some time on the cold ground. We are almost exactly the same size. Please go through the closet in your room and feel free to wear anything you'd like. We're all putting on our PJ's."

"Oh, my goodness, I don't know what to say or how to thank you."

Linda takes subtle control.

"Come with me Edna, I'll show you to your room. I think you'll like it. In the morning you'll be able to see the lake from your windows."

Edna gets settled into her very large room which is decorated in various shades of blue, Edna's favorite color. She takes a hot bath in what Edna could only describe as luxury and whispers to herself:

"Thank you Lord. Why did you do this for me? Was I a good girl all year long? She giggles with delight at her own little joke.

Downstairs in the kitchen, Richard and Kevin explain to Linda the events leading up to having Edna as a house guest. Linda smiled and threw her arms around Richard and Kevin at the same time. "I am so, so proud of both of you!" she said. "This is *truly* a special Christmas. Hey, we have finally been blessed with a Christmas guest. How about that! Let's have milk and cookies in the great room and enjoy the tree. I'll pour Edna a glass of milk too."

The family moved into the great room and set four glasses of cold milk and a dish of assorted Christmas cookies on the cherry wood coffee table. The whole room was adorned with decorations giving the room the feeling of a winter wonderland.

Edna felt wonderful. She dressed in expensive pajamas chosen from the walk-in closet. And the robe, oh the lovely, warm, and furry light blue robe which Linda had laid across the bed felt wonderful. For a brief moment Edna felt as though she may have passed away and been swept up to heaven. Again, giggling to herself with unexpected delight. She had brought her own slippers and of course, her trusty cane; then she was ready to go downstairs and join the family for Christmas Eve!

Edna walked into the great-room looking and feeling wonderful.

"I just love your tree and all the decorations!" she whispered as she glanced around the room, taking in every ounce of the holiday ambiance.

"Come on over here and sit next to me, Miss Edna," Kevin piped up and said. "This is the best view of the tree. I helped decorate it, you know."

"I'm sure you did!" Edna said, sitting down next to Kevin on the comfortable loveseat. Linda and Richard sat directly across from them on the sofa, with the cherry wood coffee table with milk and cookies placed invitingly between them.

"How was your bath, Edna," Linda asked. "Is your room okay?"

Edna wiped a tear from her eye, as she looked at Linda across the coffee table.

"Yes, she humbly said, "everything is just perfect. And, Linda, I'm am in love with this robe. Thank you. Thank you all for everything."

"Don't mention it," Richard added. "We are *elated*, *more* than glad to have you here, Edna. As you know, thanks to Kevin, we seldom if ever have guests for Christmas. Linda's parents are gone and when I found out I was adopted at the age of twenty one, it turned my world upside down.

Kevin wasn't paying attention; he'd heard it all before and just accepted the fact that his father was adopted. Heck, Kevin had a couple of friends who were adopted. It was no big deal to him.

"There was a huge argument within our family, Richard continued. "I hired a lawyer to basically *find out who I am*. He did some investigating and discovered that I was bought and paid for like a piece of furniture, but that's as far as my lawyer got. He could not find out exactly who sold me to the Hudsons, and they weren't talking."

The Hudsons? Edna froze, hoping no one would notice.

Richard continued with his story. "That infuriated me, and I left home. I never even said good-bye or looked back. I haven't seen or heard from my *parents* since, and I am forty five years old now. I'd give anything to meet my *real* parents. Someone once wrote me an anonymous letter saying that my mother died of a broken heart."

She did, thought Edna.

"It's never been proven so I choose to believe she is alive and well. No mother should have her new born baby torn from her arms and ripped from her life. It's unspeakable, and I *detest* the Hudsons for it".

Linda put her hand lovingly on Richard's trembling hand and held it there. "Honey, it's alright," she said in a soft, understanding voice, "*we* love you, and that's all that matters."

Richard always got a little melancholy on Christmas about not knowing where he really came from; but he usually gets over it quickly, changing his mood from somewhat blue to cheery, happy and thankful for Linda and Kevin. He poured himself another glass of milk.

"Here Edna, try one of these Santa Clause cookies. They're my favorite". As Richard passed the cookie plate to her, she noticed a resemblance between herself and Richard. There was something about his eyes and somewhat crooked nose, which was barely noticeable unless you were looking for it. Well, *Edna* was looking for it now, and she found it.

Oh my dear Lord, could it be?

She nearly fainted but held on to her consciousness, with a million thoughts – happy thoughts, yet melancholy and sad at the same time – going through her mind. The hour was getting late – nearly ten p.m. on Christmas Eve.

Edna ate a Santa Clause cookie and finished her milk.

"This is such a special Christmas Eve for me. You are such *wonderful* people. Kevin, give me a hug".

And he did.

"I think I'll go to bed now, and dream about sugar plums and Rudolph the Red Nosed Reindeer."

Everybody chuckled in good cheer.

Edna kissed Kevin, Linda and Richard goodnight, once again examining Richard's nose. Everyone said one last goodnight and Edna used her cane flawlessly to climb the stairs to her room.

Richard and Linda tucked Kevin into bed. They had to check on the puppy in the basement. Their plan was to get up a little earlier than Kevin and have the blonde furry puppy sitting under the tree when the little fellow came downstairs from his bedroom. It would be a memorable Christmas. No doubt about that. Kevin will also have a new baseball glove waiting for him under the tree. He'll be a happy little boy on Christmas morning, the way it should be. Richard was proud of himself for his good job and his ability to make every Christmas special for Kevin and Linda.

The puppy was fine.

Christmas Morning

Edna was up at the crack of dawn, and in an unusually high spirited mood. She had taken her shower, brushed her near perfect teeth, (like Richard's) and dried and brushed her thick salt and pepper hair. The lake view was breathtaking. She had just finished making the bed when a soft knock came to her door. She put on the light blue robe and opened it. There stood a smiling Linda with a cup of coffee in her hand.

"Merry Christmas, Edna" Linda whispered so as not to wake Kevin. "Are you ready to come down? Richard and I thought you might want to see the look on Kevin's little face when he sees his puppy for the first time."

Edna smiled wide. "I wouldn't miss it for the world. I'll be right down. Thank you, Linda, for asking me – and for bringing the coffee, too."

"Good. How do you like your coffee, Edna?"

"One lump of sugar and one squirt of milk. Thanks again, Linda."

Linda disappeared down the carpeted stair steps.

Richard had already brought the puppy up from the basement.

The big moment was near.

Edna had just arrived in the great room to find her fresh cup of coffee and a piece of apple pie waiting for her on the coffee table, a stack of holiday napkins in the middle of the table.

Richard, seated on the sofa, set his coffee cup down. "Linda, honey, I think it's time to bring Kevin down. I'm going to take some pictures and try to catch his first impressions of seeing the pup".

"Sounds like a good idea. We'll be right down. Ready, Edna?"

"I'm as ready as I'll ever be, excited, too. This is just all so, so magical. Like a pleasant dream come true,"

"Edna, keep in mind, *you* are one of the reasons it *is* such a magical Christmas, we love having you here."

The puppy, an eight week old mixed-breed bundle of fur was a male, rescued from the animal shelter. Richard and Edna played with the dog while waiting for Kevin and Linda. Edna could hold back no longer.

"So, Richard, what do you know of your biological parents."

He looked up, a bit surprised by the question.

"I really don't know very much at all," he replied, "but like I said last night, the Hudsons wouldn't tell me and my lawyer came up short."

"Richard," Edna forged on, "do you have a birth mark on your arm?"

"Uh, yes, yes I do Edna. How did *you* know? I've had long sleeve shirts and a sweater on since you've been here- you couldn't have seen it."

Richard and Edna lock eyes.

"Richard, is your birthmark shaped like a...."

Kevin arrived at the entrance of the great room and let out a scream of surprise and joy when he saw his perfect little puppy.

Richard got off about five pictures of the special moment.

Kevin gathered up the puppy in his arms, and the little dog instantly enjoyed licking Kevin's face. Kevin then spotted his new baseball glove among the other packages – a perfect Christmas indeed!

As the event calmed down a bit with Kevin sitting in the love-seat petting and talking to his new friend for life, Richard, his interest piqued by Edna's question about his birthmark began thinking.

How could she possibly know?

He stood up and beckoned Edna into the kitchen.

"How do you know about...," he somewhat anxiously asked.

Edna takes a step closer and gently reaches for Richard's hands. "Richard, is your birthmark shaped like a heart"?

Richard stood perfectly still in a strange state of conscious shock. Tears began to run down both of his cheeks.

Could it be true?

Edna was also crying the tears of joy she had longed for, prayed for, since the day they took her baby.

"May I see your birthmark? Edna asked. "I've got to be sure."

Richard nodded, and allowed Edna, *whom he now knew in his heart, was his mother*, to push up the left sleeve of his Christmas sweater.

She looked up at Richard and said, "I've missed you, son."

They embraced, and Richard cried almost uncontrollably before finally getting out the words "I've missed you too, mother." Still sobbing with utter, indescribable joy, Richard gently locked his arm with his mother's, much like a proud new husband and wife walking down the aisle at their wedding.

"Shall we dry our tears before going back in?"

"Yes, just give me a moment to gather myself…son."

Linda, wondering what Richard and Edna were doing in the kitchen for so long, was on the verge of walking in to check, when Richard and Edna came walking arm in arm back into the great room. Linda and Kevin looked up at them in silence. Richard's voice was loud, happy and filled with emotion. Looking adoringly at his mother, and then turning to face his wife and son with a huge smile on his handsome face, he made the big announcement.

"Edna and I have something to tell you."

Author Bio:

Nelson Trout is a singer/song writer who lives in New Jersey. Of late, he has turned his creative talents toward prose. His latest book, Raven April, was published by Fireside Publications and can be found on the publisher's website, *www.firesidepubs.com* as well as on Kindle and Nook. He is currently working on a sequel which has been tentatively titled Raven Returns. Also, look for Nelson's musical-poem on page 67 of this anthology.

Taking Miss Minnie Home
by
Jackie Grommes

They're an odd pair, Sis and Miss Minnie. Miss Minnie barely makes an outline under her bedcovers. Her tiny grandma-body is lost beneath a utilitarian sheet and well-worn quilt. A shock of white hair surrounds her angular face and fans out on the pillow.

In a bed close by is her roommate – a formidable woman whose body doesn't work well anymore, but whose heart is always available for the taking. That woman is my sister.

I visit her weekly at Green Oaks Nursing Home which has neither oaks nor much green, for that matter. I share family news and the latest pictures of my grandchildren who are also hers, at least in spirit. Our animated voices sound odd among the steady cacophony of call bells and rolling carts in the halls.

Sis has a puckered look on her face if I start to laugh too loudly as I have been known to snort at inappropriate times, something that she considers very unladylike. We make fun of silly reality shows (which we watch religiously) and wonder about why my "kids" don't call often enough. With self-righteousness befitting proper Southern women, we are firm in the memory that we called *our* momma every Sunday evening no matter what we were doing. If there is a momentary silence it is comfortable - there is a lot that is unspoken between sisters who have so much history between them.

Miss Minnie is only a few feet away but she doesn't interfere in our visits. She is the perfect nursing home roommate. She doesn't turn her TV up to the highest setting and then fall asleep or squabble about Sis's things encroaching on her space. Sis's corner is a duplicate of all the rooms of her life - family pictures and knickknacks cover every available surface. Progressive crayon drawings from beloved nieces and nephews adorn the walls. Small angels and other gifts are crowded on the dresser tops. The fading 8x10 picture of Mom and Dad taken years ago for the Methodist Church Directory is prominently displayed.

Our beloved parents died within a few months of each other and left Sis bereft and unable to continue in the normal world. The grief from that loss overwhelmed her so completely that her mind and body failed in concert and left me this replacement sister to care for. The last time she fell in my home she laid hopelessly on the floor not caring if anyone came to pick her up or not. After a flurry of long distance phone calls with my other sisters, we moved her and her little nest of pictures and mementos to Green Oaks.

There in the modest room that is now my sister's home, we sometimes talk in whispers about Miss Minnie and look forward to celebrating her 100th birthday on Christmas Day. If Miss Minnie had her way, the guest of honor would be conspicuously absent for the occasion, however. The truth of the matter is she refuses to allow anything in her space that implies that she might be at Green Oaks for any length of time at all. There are no children's pictures, no angel collection. Her little closet is full of the gifts that she has been given and are boxed and waiting to go home with her. In spite of this mandate, a glittery "Jesus is the Reason for the Season" sign has been allowed to dangle crookedly on the wall across from her bed. Christmas decorations are the exception to Miss Minnie's rule for they have a short lifespan anyway, and do not imply that she will be a resident here for the rest of her life.

Who knows why these two unlikely women became friends. During the long gap between lunch and dinner, Miss Minnie sits in her wheelchair next to Sis's bed and tells her about her days as a young, full-blood Indian wife. She speaks the ancient language fluently when a tribal member comes to visit. She often talks about the old traditions and recites her Indian Roll Number proudly.

Sis tells her about working for many years as a secretary at the imposing and prestigious Calvary Presbyterian Church and then taking care of our aging parents until they passed away. I suppose they both live in the past a bit. It happens as we get older and have less and less to look forward to.

Mostly Miss Minnie talks about going home. When she first came to "The Home" as *we* came to call it, she fretted about what would happen to her beloved possessions that remained unprotected in her modest house on the reservation. Ms. Gloria Tallgrass, her attorney and friend, promised the worried little woman that her lifetime accumulation of pottery and family turquoise were being watched over by vigilant neighbors. But as she worked the edge of her quilt with arthritic fingers,

Miss Minnie's pursed lips and silent stare spoke volumes about her lack of confidence in that statement.

Ms. Tallgrass helped Miss Minnie in every way that she could, however, she was never able to grant her friend's coveted wish that she would be able to go home. Surprisingly vocal when she needed to be, the normally reserved Miss Minnie complained bitterly to her doctor (and anyone else that would listen) that she was capable of being home alone. But it must have seemed to her that no one listened because soon she stopped complaining.

It was painful passing through Miss Minnie's plain little space to sit in the uncomfortable chair next to Sis's bed among the menagerie of memories.

"I'm going home soon," Miss Minnie would say with a big smile. "I'll be there for my birthday on Christmas Day."

I would smile back and nod, not knowing what the proper response should be. That topic wasn't addressed in the *Welcome to Green Oaks!* orientation booklet I got when I moved Sis in. Sis often said the same thing about going home until she got used to being waited on and decided she would settle in and go for it.

But it was Miss Minnie's mantra and it broke my heart.

Sis and I would talk about "the Miss Minnie's situation" often. We knew from conversations we overheard that she had life insurance proceeds in the bank and could afford to hire a full time caretaker. We also wondered why the Tribe couldn't use casino proceeds to hire a companion for Miss Minnie. She just wanted to live her last bit of time on earth in the cheery little rooms where she had cooked for Earl, night after night for over fifty years. It was where they shared their days until he died in his sleep and left her in the little house alone. One day she fell and broke her hip, starting the slide down the slippery slope that led to Green Oaks.

I often fantasized about taking Miss Minnie and all her boxed up gifts and caring for her on the reservation. I would put up a small Christmas tree with lots of twinkling white lights. I would help her to the shower and tuck her into the little bed she had shared with Earl all those years. I would be good company for her and in the evenings she would tell me about growing up on the reservation and how the young people today are marrying outside of the Tribe, as she often did when we visited with her.

My Sunday evenings were still reserved for family telephone calls but they were now with my normal sister, Joy, who lives in

California. She was very familiar with "the Miss Minnie situation" as she had been here to visit Sis and fell for the charming Miss Minnie the way everyone does. I reminded her that Miss Minnie's 100th birthday was coming up soon, so she planned her next visit to coincide with what was sure to be a great party in the dining room of Green Oaks.

I could picture Miss Minnie in her wheelchair with her impressive white hair brushed neatly, wearing a flowered dress that Ms. Tallgrass would purchase downtown at Sadie's for Ladies. I would buy her a fragrant corsage that would be from Sis and me. It would overpower her little body, but it would show off how much she was loved by someone.

Joy and I had been talking a lot about what gift to get this sweet, soon to be centenarian for her birthday when we hatched "the plan." After Miss Minnie's celebrated birthday party, we would take her home in her wheelchair and stay with her. It would be our gift to the very special Miss Minnie. We would trade off days and nights, cooking and cleaning, trips to the doctor. We were two bright, resourceful women and we could do anything we set our minds to. Between us we had raised five children, guided husbands through mid-life crises, alcoholism, job losses and baldness. We were no strangers to life's challenges and we were cheered by the thought of making Miss Minnie happy at last. We *were* respectable women after all, so we would go through the proper channels but if thwarted, we would just break her out and wheel her away. What could they do, arrest us? We were unstoppable.

It was the Sunday before Christmas and I had picked up Sis's favorite take out meal - a Sonic cheeseburger, fries and diet Dr. Pepper with cherry flavoring. I entered Green Oaks through the back entrance as usual. Tacky gold and green garland fluttered around an old recycled wreath as I opened the door greeted by the usual antiseptic smell. I could see a commotion around Sis's door and I must have had a panicked look on my face because a nurse quickly assured me that Sis was fine. Then I saw the nurse's aide going down the hall doing the "just closin' the doors for a minute, hon," routine. That was the tell-tale sign of a death in The Home.

I'm certain that I will never forget the events of that day. They come to me in slow motion with everyone moving heavily, frame by frame. The coroner filed out, all business. The gurney followed with the tiny figure of Miss Minnie and her pretty hair covered for the last time with a heavy white sheet. Following her was the solemn group of

Indian men and women whom I had seen visiting with her after services on Sundays. Resigned nursing home personnel looked away sadly and didn't make eye contact with me. Sis sobbed quietly at the loss of her friend while the Nursing Home Director asked her if she wanted to be taken out of the room for awhile. She didn't and I went toward the room to console her.

Then I spotted Ms. Gloria Tallgrass, attorney and friend. I stammered a phrase I had heard on TV crime shows, "sorry for your loss," or something equally as inane. She smiled at me through tears.

"You should be happy, she finally got her wish."

"Her wish?" I asked. I looked at Ms. Tallgrass as though she had just grown another head. "Miss Minnie finally got her wish," she said.

"She finally got to go home."

Author Bio:

Jackie moved to St. Augustine three years ago to be near family and rekindled her love of writing. Her short story, "The Christmas Table" was published in Snowbird Christmas Vol. 2 and "Going Home" was published in the Florida Writer/Spring 2013. She is currently working on a collection of children's stories. Jackie can be reached at jgrommes@spinn.net.

MARY CHRISTMAS

He spun his dreidel, ate chocolate gelt,
then deep within his holiday heart, he felt
a penchant to paint us a Christmas tree,
share his joy and make us merry.
He signed off with a note.
"Mary Christmas," he wrote.

My muse, our grandson, six years old,
inspired gratitude that should be told. . .

Thank you Mary Christmas
for tendering Baby Jesus.
Saint Joseph did what he could
to seek shelter so you would
be protected for your delivery trial.
Alleluia to your newborn child.

Thank you Mary Christmas.

New Year's Resolutions
by
Don Lubov

Resolutions come and go,
At lightening speed they're gone.

Intentions matter not at all,
Sincerity's hither and yon.

Age is not a factor, too,
For all resolves do pale.

Doomed from the start, a promise made,
Will ultimately fail.

"Why?" you ask. "Can this be so."
Said not with tongue in cheek.

Because you see, right from the start,
The will to win is weak.

I know. I know. You think I give
A biased sort of rot.
But trust me when I tell you that
My vision's tainted not.

Even you, a skeptic ear,
Detects a statement true.

But take not my word as a proof.
Experiment on you.

Resolve to be or do a thing,

A change you find appealing.

And see if you can make it so.
With little wheeling-dealing.

If you can succeed in this,
Where many more have failed.

You deserve applause and more,
Your efforts should be hailed.

But if you try and cannot win.
You've proved a message well.

And you will be like most of us,
Who tried to rise but fell.

You'll sing our song of resolutions,
Made with zeal and hope.

That failed with efforts small and great,
And forced us all to cope.

With less than perfect scores accrued,
Resigned to try again.

So here's to you and us and them,
All women and all men.

Hope springs eternal at this time,
Don't let us be the breakers.

Hang in there and try once more,
You resolution makers.

My New Year's Resolutions 2000

by
Trudi

Retirement had been good to me. From the snow-bound North, I found sunny Central Florida with all its gated communities and golf courses. Whatever activity I desired, was available.

After a few years, I became bored with having no one-person relationship for those special moments in life. My family, friends and a plethora of social activities kept me busy with a very desirable lifestyle, but that special someone just wasn't there.

I never had a desire to go *looking for a man,* as many women in my social circle did; I never felt the need to have a man just for the sake of having a man; I was self-sufficient, but now a nagging loneliness had begun to set in. I didn't want marriage – had already failed at that – I wanted a companion, someone special in my life – not a sex-partner, just someone special to share those special moments in my life.

New Years Eve, 2000 had arrived; a new year –a new century – and I was feeling pensive – alone in a crowd. Without thinking much about it, I took out a pen and paper and began to write:

New Year's Resolutions for 2000

- *I want to meet a man; someone who cares about me, just for me*
- *He must be willing to accept me for myself – just as I am*
- *He should enjoy dining out occasionally and picking up the check*
- *He should enjoy some social activities – dancing, theater, golf and a bit of traveling, but not be consumed by it*
- *He should be cooperative and accept my wacky family when the need arises, trying though it may be*
- *Financially well-off and generous would be nice tho not the most important aspects*
- *Reasonably good looks and good health would be ideal.*

As a friend approached to ask me to dance the *Moonlight Dance* at the dawn of a new year, I quickly tore off my written note and tucked it safely in a small zippered section of my purse. Then I danced in the New Year, complete with the obligatory kiss to end another perfect evening.

Several months later I found the note intact just where I had placed it.

Hmmm, I thought, and giggled as I remembered the evening. *Guess that didn't work so well.* And with just a tad of superstition, perhaps even hope, I returned the Resolution Note to its resting place in the side pocket of my occasionally used purse. Through the next couple of years, that action was repeated several times with little thought given to it.

In the Spring of 2001, my friend Lila, who was always trying to pair me off with someone, excitedly told me about a new man in the community. She and her husband had played golf with him the previous day.

"There's just one thing wrong with him," she said, but all the women are flexing their muscles to go after him. You'd better throw your hat in the ring."

I laughed.

"Not me, I said. "If I have to chase him down, I don't want him. I can't compete with those ladies, anyway; they have a lot more practice than I do."

Lila looked at me with that disgusted look that only she has perfected.

"For Christ, sake!" she scowled. If you keep this up, you're never going to find a man here. Do you want to be alone for the rest of your life?"

"Fine with me," I replied. "It's worked well for a long time. Besides, you said there's something wrong with this guy. What is it?"

"He's nice looking, but he's a little paunchy – with a pot belly. But I hear he's a millionaire," she quickly added.

"Only you, Lila, would focus on the *pot belly*. Enough of this chatter," I said. "I have work to do. Guess I should admit that I did take your advice and asked Greg at the Pro Shop to let me know if anyone needed a golf partner so I could play golf with you and Len more often. Don't know if anything will come of it."

"Well, at least that's something," she pouted as she moved toward her golf cart to leave." Just to get the last word in, she added, "By the way, his name is Bill – just in case…"

Three days later, my doorbell rang. There stood a paunchy seventy-year-old man with a slight pot belly.

"Hi, my name is Bill. I just wanted to introduce myself. Greg said you might be looking for a golf partner…"

Thus began the best 12-year relationship of my life.

Gosh, I miss you, Bill.

And my family, adults and children alike, still reflect on their fond memories of "Grandpa Bill."

Elm &Lobster Trap

Part Three

Holidays of Springtime & Summer

Celebrating: Rebirth, Renewal & Independence

The Essence of Spring

San Juan's Jewell

St. Joe's spring fiesta is in the air.
Tourists, townfolk gather to bear
witness at San Juan, California's
Mission--Capistrano. There'll be a

migration--a bevy of Argentina's swallows.
Birds leave their Corrientes cliff hollows,
wing 6,000 miles north in early spring.
Swiftly build mud nests which cling

to the ruins of this quaint stone church.
Along Capistrano's arches they perch.
The Chapel is exposed as the roof fell
in the earthquake of eighteen twelve.

Every year on October twenty third
each and every vacationing bird
takes flight, en masse, circling
the Mission in farewell bidding.

The fluttering coastal cloud wings home.
Next spring this miracle again will come,
delight the crowds who gather as one,
at the Jewel of Missions-Capistrano.

A Marti Gras' Happening
The Wicked Witch Murder

by
Linda Lehmann Masek

The reason that Richard Blaney's wife, Vivienne, was murdered, was because his high-priced black Cadillac broke down. Completely, totally and unexpectedly broke down, causing Richard to leave his car in the repair shop in uptown New Orleans and take the St. Charles Streetcar home. Upon arriving at Blaney and Blaney, Inc., Funeral Home and mortician's residence bordering the Garden District and the downtown French Quarter, Richard exited the street car and traipsed through the fresh, dew soaked walkway to his own front door, past blossoming blood-red azaleas and ochre rhododendrons that showered their blossoms over his dark gray, conservative business suit. He let himself in quietly through the front stucco door of the gingerbread-style funeral home and proceeded past the small chapel, Viewing Room Number One, to the stairs leading to the basement.

This particular late morning found Richard Blaney more than a little annoyed with the world in general, not just because his new car had broken down, but because, as an embalmer and mortician he had a corpse to prepare for the evening visitation. The fact that the corpse had turned out to be an old and dear friend, who was exactly the same age as Richard, didn't help his mood in the slightest. Bob Grafton had literally keeled over in the prime of life. As Richard slipped a white lab coat and apron over his dark gray shirt and slacks, he walked over to the stainless steel embalming table and studied poor Bob dispassionately.

They had attended the same high school and played on the same Louisiana football team in college, and looked as alike as twin peas out of the same pod. Richard pulled white latex gloves on over dark brown, muscular hands before trying to arrange Bob's mouth in some semblance of a smile. Richard thought about the resemblance between them as he massaged Bob's arms and legs to relieve the rigor mortis before making a small incision with his knife to officially begin the embalming process, i.e. the drawing of blood from the body and replacing it with a pinkish embalming fluid before aspirating the chest cavity.

Richard began to sweat, despite the cool, antiseptic-like atmosphere in the basement. His wife, Vivienne, called the embalming room a morgue and wouldn't come near the place. But Richard, who had inherited the business from Richard Blaney, Senior, long deceased, normally enjoyed his work and liked to present his clients in as lifelike a position as possible, which pleased their relatives and kept his business going strong.

As Richard sat down on the hard metal-backed chair that grated into his spine, he thought once again about the wisdom of opening a branch of Blaney's in the capital, Baton Rouge. Granted, it would be more work, but business had been booming, and the natives of New Orleans, who had always seemed to Richard to be overly concerned with death, would welcome an addition. As he carefully washed the blood from poor Bob's naked body before dressing him in the black suit and white tie his family had provided, Richard had pretty much decided to open the Baton Rouge Funeral Home. He then applied special cosmetics to Bob's frozen features; this had always been Richard's favorite part of the entire procedure. Suddenly he heard a door slam somewhere in the funeral parlor upstairs.

That would be his wife, Vivienne, who also managed the business part of Blaney and Blaney, such as publicity and taxes, finally getting to work after meeting with those loopy friends of hers. Richard frowned as he accidently smeared a bit of the cosmetic on Bob's jawline and had to make a re-do. Since Vivienne hated the embalming room and definitely wouldn't come down, he should probably go up and at least tell her he had returned home, inasmuch as his car wasn't in its customary space. Unfortunately, just thinking about where she had been really soured his mood and turned him off.

Another door slammed upstairs, making Richard jump. His wife had her twice-weekly Wicked Witches Society Meetings on Tuesday and Thursday, where a group of what Richard privately considered to be wackos discussed all things "witchy" in New Orleans. When Richard had met Vivienne, shortly after his divorce from first wife, Mary, he had been delighted with her interest in everything from French pralines and the French Creoles who lived in the Quarter. When this interest had extended to the Wicked Witches and consisted in midnight meetings on All Hallow's Eve or numerous other times throughout the year, Richard voiced his displeasure. Vivienne had looked horrified at Richard when he suggested she take up some other hobby to occupy her time since he would appreciate his wife being home at night.

Richard finally finished arranging poor Bob tidily in the casket his family had picked out at Blaney and Blaney's casket-selection room. He wiped his forehead free of sweat and made a last check. Bob looked so lifelike, it was hard to believe he had died. An A-one job. Richard smiled and patted himself on the back. He had just turned away when the telephone jingled in his wife's business office upstairs. He heard the dorky little ring complete with song she had added and took a step toward the extension 'phone in the basement.

Richard picked up the telephone, his curiosity rampant as to who might be calling his wife. His ex-wife Mary had accused him of being jealous, which could be true, since Vivienne was twenty years younger and gorgeous with her long, blonde hair, green-flecked tiger eyes and model's figure. Richard knew many of his friends thought Vivienne had married him for his money. Why else would she have embraced the partially bald, heavy-set, running to fat funeral director as her husband? Regardless, he hesitated only a moment and picked up the telephone, expecting to hear the middle-aged voice of a Wicked Witch on the other end of the line.

Instead smooth as silk tones, obviously male, came to his ear. Richard almost dropped the 'phone.

"Am I going to see you later? I wasn't sure when you'd be back again!"

Vivienne's voiced responded.

"I can't get away until tomorrow. But I'll call you. I don't want to get caught and spoil everything!"

Richard could feel the color leave his face as the dorky kid muttered, "O.K.," and rang off. He stood still, holding the 'phone in shock and stared at it wordlessly as Vivienne hung up. He heard her high heels moving around upstairs, as he slowly and methodically replaced the receiver.

So that's how she had been spending her time! With a lover..or worse! Richard felt his stomach churn and almost didn't make the bathroom before he vomited. Vivienne was a piece of trash like his first wife; he had heard her making a rendezvous with his own ears! His body shook like he had St. Vitus' Dance. This was how she respected her marriage vows! Her and that...words failed Richard as he called the young Romeo every four letter word he had ever heard quietly under his breath. Even worse for Richard, his friends and even his ex-wife had been right when they claimed Vivienne married him for his money, a gold digger, nothing more, nothing less!

Richard barely heard the outside door slam as Vivienne left. Probably to join her Wicked Witch cronies. And she had teased him about being a ghoul because of his work in the basement!

Richard carefully sponged off his face and grasped the sink for support. Vivienne would be gone for awhile, so he would have a chance to pull himself together. And the answer? A divorce? Probably, but...Richard felt the heat of white-hot anger begin churning up his stomach all over again! He left and sat by poor Bob, lying in his casket, quiet, at peace, so at home. Perhaps poor Bob was the lucky one! Richard sat down and put his hand on his old friend. One marriage, a couple of kids, a loyal wife. Why did some guys have all the luck and others, like him, end up with nothing, despite their best efforts?

Richard leaned his head down in his hands. I wonder what he looks like, he thought to himself, this man who had taken Vivienne from him. He had sounded young on the telephone. Was he blonde like Vivienne, or dark? He had spoken with a slight accent that could have been French. And his face... all of a sudden, Richard felt consumed with a desire to know. Then, as he stared at Bob's peaceful face devoid of care, he remembered the security tapes.

Blaney and Blaney had had trouble with vandals, especially at Halloween and Mardi Gras time, when the college kids moved in on New Orleans to eat, drink, be merry and drink a lot more. Richard had finally installed three security cameras covering the front entranceway after a rock with the word "ghoul" on it in red paint had come hurtling through his front window. Unfortunately, the tapes had to be checked and changed at regular intervals. But if Vivienne had seen her friend earlier this week...

Richard attacked the security camera concealed in the front closet of Blaney and Blaney like it was a creature to be destroyed, slamming the two-day old tape back to the beginning of the day and fast-forwarding it through the previous hours. He had pretty much given up, when he saw them and pushed at the stop button. Richard reversed and saw Vivienne in a lime-green, spring dress with green spotted heels, purse dangling, tripping down their front walk and mincing over to the dark-colored van parked at the gate. Richard stared as he played back the rendezvous in real time. He saw the driver lean over to open the door and stopped the picture on his face. The driver looked young, muscular, and good-looking, with a roughness totally lacking in

Richard. He smiled a sexy, come-hither smile at Vivienne, as she slid into the front seat of the van. Richard squinted as the two heads came together. Blast it, he couldn't see! Were they kissing? Was her young lover raining kisses up and down her throat? After long moments, the van pulled away; Richard slammed his hand into the screen causing the picture to go black.

The final piece of evidence of his wife's perfidy! He had seen it with his own eyes! A divorce? There was no question! Should he confront her? But why? Why listen to her try and lie her way out?

Richard felt the flame of fury grow in his belly. Then he thought again of poor Bob, still in his casket in the basement, and an idea germinated. She should pay, Richard thought. He had lived with her, shared his wealth with her, loved her with his whole heart and soul, and she had betrayed him! But she would pay!

Bob's relatives wouldn't be arriving until early evening. Vivienne would surely come home in the meantime. When she did...he would be ready!

Richard set Bob's casket in Viewing Room Number One and artfully arranged his flowers. The spray from his wife covered half of the casket, while Mark and Angel, his two children, each had rose baskets alongside. Bob's parents had sent flowers along with numerous friends, business and otherwise; so many Richard assumed Bob had been a popular man.

Then Richard doused the lights in the room except for the two tall taper-candles at each end of the casket. They supplied enough light to move around, but not enough to clearly see that poor Bob wasn't in his casket as planned. Richard, dressed in his best black suit and white tie, had artfully applied the mortuary cosmetics to his own face, and now waited quietly by the window. When at least he saw Vivienne's bright red Corvette Stingray pull through the gates, Richard went back and crawled beneath the spray of flowers.

He heard her key in the lock and the sound of his wife's heels tapping across the floor as she came in.

"Richard?" Her voice, low and delightfully musical to the ear, filled him with repugnance. He closed his eyes and breathed as little as possible.

Vivienne Blaney saw the sign, Robert Grafton, and eased herself slowly into the room. It reeked of flowers: the two candle torches glowed weirdly in the semi-darkness. She peered toward the casket and gave a start; her husband had commented the night before on his likeness to the dead man. Vivienne turned to go, but then her eyes widened as she stared hard at the corpse. She thought, for just a moment, that she had seen poor Bob breathe!

No, it's the light, she told herself mentally. The woman licked her lips and drew closer. Her feet seemed to move of their own volition, one step after another, past the reeking flowers and to the casket.

She stared down, the candle light throwing the rest of the room into silhouette and making deep shadows on the corpse. It seemed uncanny; he really did look like her husband, alive and well. And then the breath caught in her throat, as his chest moved. Tiger-flecked green eyes widened as she gazed transfixed. And yet she couldn't turn her eyes away!

She moved closer still and put out a tentative hand to touch the corpse. Vivienne had never been able to touch the dead, in spite of the fact that she had been around dead people the entire five years that she and Richard had been married. To her sorrow, she did so now. The head of the corpse turned and he sat up and reached out to grasp her arm.

Her scream of terror resounded throughout the room and would have been loud enough to wake poor Bob, lounging temporarily in the distant coat room. When the corpse stared with blackened eyes into her soul, Vivienne turned, yanked her arm away, thrashed toward the door, slipped on her heel and crashed to the floor. She dragged herself half-erect, crawling toward the entrance. The corpse sat still as she stumbled again and smacked into a decorative urn standing by the window. It weaved crazily back and forth. Her shrill scream pierced the air again as the corpse swung itself out of the casket. Vivienne's breath stopped in her throat; she grabbed her chest as shooting pains started running down her arms and she keeled over.

Richard knelt by his wife's side; the mortuary cosmetics smeared against his pale, grotesque face. He touched his wife's hand; it was cold and without the vibrant life he had so loved. Richard leaned back in shock; he had seen enough dead people to guess what had happened. And the police confirmed it after he replaced poor Bob in his casket, removed the cosmetics from his face and finally called them.

Vivienne made a beautiful corpse. Richard looked down at the prize which had escaped his grasp. His skill had made her seem lifelike; it appeared as though she still lived. Everyone thought so and sympathized with him as eyes gushing with crocodile tears, he proclaimed his love long and loud. Her parents, her younger brother, her sisters, all came to pay their respects. The Wicked Witches chanted prayer-like in a circle around the casket with candles lit and tears in their eyes, sniffling loudly. The heart attack that had claimed Vivienne had taken her away from all of them.

Richard played his role well as the sorrowing widower, shook hands, murmured condolences to Vivienne's family, commented on how really beautiful she appeared. He had talked to her sobbing mother and in-shock father when he looked up and saw him.

It was the kid from the tape, the guy Vivienne had been seeing behind his back! The young lover come to see the adulteress. Richard almost rubbed his eyes; he couldn't believe the nerve of the guy! There was no mistake. The tape had been too clear.

What to do since the slimy little worm had had the utter gall to come here in person? Richard met him at the door, grasped the hand held out in friendship and literally dragged the little turd back out the stucco doorway and onto the stoop.

It must have dawned on the guy that this was a bit odd, even for a grieving husband. He yanked back and twisted away to confront Richard.

"Look, man. I came to tell you I'm sorry for your loss. My name is Sloan Summers and I knew your wife quite well."

"I'll just bet you did," Richard mocked him. "What are you here for? To see her for the last time? To see your lover before she makes her final trip to the crypt?"

Richard's voice had risen, but he didn't care. People stared out of the gingerbread-styled windows at the drama being played out on the porch, but his whole attention centered on the piece of slime in front of him.

Sloan Summers looked very blank.

"Yo, man, I know you're in shock. We all are. She had a beautiful body. But…"

"And naturally you'd know all about that, too!" Richard growled, holding himself in check with a mighty effort.

"Of course I would. I teach ballroom dance and…oh, I guess it doesn't matter now. Vivienne wanted to surprise you. She knew you liked to dance the old-fashioned dances as she put it, and her being so much younger, she just knew the modern stuff. So she hired me to teach her. We met at the Sloan Summer's Dance Studio three times a week. She has been practicing for months to surprise you and …"

Richard thought back to the conversation on the 'phone, to the van. "And that was all? Just…dancing?"

Sloan Summers nodded. "Right, man. Now you've got the whole scene. By the by, I'm sorry it didn't work out. She had some of the best moves. She floated. And with a weak heart, too."

Sloan Summers stopped in consternation as Richard Blaney, of Blaney and Blaney, Inc., Funeral Homes and mortician's residence broke into loud, raucous laughter. He laughed and laughed, until finally the tears started to ooze from his eyes and he collapsed on the floor. A doctor was summoned. As the tears fell and the doctor stepped over him in an unprecedented house call, a hypodermic loaded with tranquillizer was plunged into Richard's arm. Before the darkness claimed him, Richard had one final thought: the Wicked Witches had had the last laugh after all.

Author Bio:

About the Author: Linda Lehmann Masek is a teacher-librarian with advanced degrees from Cleveland State and Case-Western Reserve universities. Her diverse writing talents are shown in the differing genres of her previous books. She has penned more than 100 newspaper and journal articles in addition to contributing content to the nonfiction *AT&T Pioneer Memory Book and Encyclopedia.* An accomplished artist, pianist and photographer, Linda has written several children's books and novels. The Sea Serpent, a novel with a Florida setting is available on Fireside Publication's website, www.firesidepubs.com and on Amazon/Kindle.

Heart Probe

A valentine visit to my heart
Doctor checks every working part
Sounds surreal thru the stethoscope
EKG endorses a longevity hope

Valves are valiant; they open, shut
Aortic and mitral make the cut
Four chambers coalesce in my heart
All cooperate, comport their part

This holiday, I'll garnish 'n gild
With ruffles, glitter till it's all filled
Add Valentine notes, Cupid's token
Butterfly bandage where it's broken

Goose Talk
by
Linda Lehmann Masek

The dark eyes attached to the long, skinny, black neck peered at her over the top of the tombstone. Monica Roman tore her eyes away from the grave of her young son. The tears clouding her blue-gray eyes evaporated and she half-smiled as she looked at the bird solemnly regarding her.

"Hello, Dolly."

The goose turned, almost as though the animal actually understood her speech. Well, maybe she did, Monica thought to herself. She had been coming here for the last five years, over her lunch breaks from work, after school, whenever. The geese returned here every year from the far north during the spring school holiday to lay eggs, raise their young and thrive during the warm months of the summer. The birds seemed to really love people and perhaps the geese really did understand after all this time when they appeared every year to give birth. They certainly had been a comfort to her over the long trying weeks following her son's death. Monica often thought that animals understood far more than human beings gave them credit for, and Dolly seemed a perfect example of this.

Monica furtively wiped her eyes again. Dolly, the "goose guard" peered cautiously around the corner of the headstone. Monica was alone except for the tall, dark man in the green corduroy jacket a couple of rows over. The goose turned, honked noisily and then led the procession of geese over to the bread that Monica had left surreptitiously under the nearby willow tree.

As she watched the geese pulling the bread apart, Monica thought back to her son. Mark had loved to watch the birds, too; she looked back fondly on the times she had taken the little boy to the park and seen his eyes light up as his "friends", the geese, came to visit.

Her eyes teared again and she sniffed noisily. As Monica reached into the pocket of her car coat for a tissue, she heard someone clear his throat. The sound came almost at her elbow.

"Excuse me, but are you O.K.?" The voice was deep and well-modulated. She turned slowly. It was the dark-haired guy in the corduroy coat.

His face half-flushed almost in embarrassment as though his asking had somehow intruded on her grief.

"Yes, I'm fine." Monica hastily jammed the tissue back in her pocket. "But thank you for asking. My little boy..." she waved vaguely in the direction of the grave, "is buried here. He died of neuroblastoma almost five years ago...almost to the day. I come here often."

"Cancer," the man nodded. "It's always bad, especially with children. I come.." he nodded toward the double headstone several rows back," to see my grandparents. I've noticed you before. And them." His eyes found the geese.

The two watched the birds pulling on the bread silently for several minutes.

"It's strange. Sometimes when I come, it seems as though they are trying to comfort me, trying to talk." Monica paused. "I mean, they do communicate with each other. Dolly is the guard. She watches while the other eat, so nobody can sneak up on them. And when they are ready to fly, the leaders make a kind of 'weep, weep' sound before they take off. When one of them spots food, they honk to let the others in the flock know it is there, and they land." She paused for breath. The man definitely looked interested in what she was saying. The dark pinpricks of light in his eyes followed Monica as she turned away from the geese.

"Just be careful nobody sees you feed them. The cemetery people don't like them and somebody might complain. Oh, not me," he half-stammered as she looked askance at him. "I enjoy having them around. Something alive in this valley of the dead. But not everyone feels that way." He hesitated as though he wanted to say something more, shifting almost awkwardly on his feet. "Well, I'd better go. I need to get back to work. Maybe I'll see you again soon?"

Monica half-smiled. "I'm sure. I'm a teacher over at Woodbridge. I went back to college and got my certification after ..." she paused and bit her lip.

"Right."

Her eyes followed him as he walked slowly to his car, a black jeep parked on the steep incline of the hill. He turned and waved once before climbing into the car and pulling away.

Monica turned back to the geese. Goose talk? Weep and honk? The guy likely thought she was some kind of crackpot. What had possessed her to chatter on like that?

Then she looked at Dolly and the rest of the flock pecking happily away at the rest of the bread. Monica thought of the comfort the animals had offered her over the past five years. Suddenly, she didn't care what the attractive stranger thought. They were her friends, for better or for worse, and she was glad to have had them.

The following Saturday, Monica approached the gravesite once more. No jeep was parked on the incline. Her eyes searched the stones. And no geese either. She got out of her Chevy and wandered slowly up the hill to Mark's gravesite.

The day was warm, early in spring. The flowers she'd planted at the holiday time had taken root and the yellow daffodils had just started to bloom. It was a time of love and rebirth as the world came alive once more after the cold, stark days of winter.

Monica heard the faint rustling before she saw the geese, waddling up the hill in single file. She opened the tote bag and pulled out the bread she'd tucked inside.

They had come to keep her company after all. But, where was Dolly? Monica stared at the group looking for her favorite. Another goose stood guard, his long black neck turning from side-to-side to warn the flock of any approaching humans. But Dolly was missing!

Monica waited an extra five minutes, but Dolly didn't appear. Well, maybe the bird had gotten fed elsewhere. It was strange, because she had been with the flock for years. But...

Monica said a silent goodbye to Mark and eased back down the hill to her car. It was Saturday and no school. The day dragged before her with nothing to do. Maybe she could go wander in the mall for a while; it was as good a way as any to kill time.

Monica started her car and drove back toward the cemetery gate. She was watching for other cars when she glanced idly at the large-sized ditch. And she saw her!

Dolly lay half in the ditch and half outside of it, not moving. If Monica hadn't been driving so slowly, she would never have seen the bird. Monica knew in that moment that Dolly had been hurt.

Monica swung the car to the side of the road and rushed over. The goose raised her head, but didn't try to move away as the woman dropped to her side.

The bird had been grazed by a car. Her wing had been partially torn and her leg was hurt too! Monica gathered Dolly up in her arms; she looked away, hoping to see another car with people who might help. The road remained empty.

What to do? She couldn't leave the bird. Not after Dolly had kept her company through the many dark times in the last five years. But where to take her? Monica was a teacher, not a vet. And a vet was what she needed!

As Monica struggled to her car with Dolly in her arms, she remembered the sign. Dr. John Carpenter, DVM. A vet located back on the road crisscrossing toward the cemetery. A vet who could help and who wouldn't, hopefully, think she'd gone crazy for spending time and money on a wild bird.

"He'll help us, Dolly. He has to. I can't lose you the way I lost Mark."

Dolly looked at her from the front seat of the car as Monica burned rubber leaving the cemetery. She spun the car back to the vet's office, exited the vehicle and rushed to his door.   Let him have office hours today. Please let him be here!

Monica yanked on the door and almost fell into the room. The receptionist looked up as she rushed to the desk.

"Please. I have a goose with me. She was hit by a car and I wondered…could the vet take a look? I can pay…"

"No problem." The receptionist had straight, lanky hair and buck teeth, but to Monica, right then, she'd become the most beautiful person on the earth. "Do you need help getting her in here?"

"No. I'm just…"   Monica felt her eyes fill with tears. She brushed them angrily away. "I'm sort of strung out. I can get her."

Monica hurried back to the car, gently picked Dolly up and carried her inside. The receptionist guided her into one of the examining rooms before she left.

"It will be fine, Dolly. The doctor can help you. You'll see. It will be fine."

Monica hoped she was right. Wild birds were strange creatures. Sometimes it was almost impossible to help them, mainly because they often had an inherent distrust of people in general.

Monica heard the door open and shut. She turned and felt the surprise which was mirrored in her face.

"It's you!" she stuttered at the dark, attractive man from the cemetery, now in the white lab coat of a veterinarian. "You're…"

"Dr. Carpenter." He held out a hand, the surprise also apparent in his face. "The goose lady," and he half-smiled, "with a patient."

Monica looked back to Dolly. "I think a car grazed her. It's her wing and one leg." She stopped, biting her lip.

Dr. Carpenter carefully eased close to Dolly and gently lifted the leg and wing. "It's not broken," he finally said. "She's got some torn tissue, but there's no break. I'll take an x-ray and keep her overnight. But..she should be fine!"

Monica felt the tears start. "Thank you. I'm so grateful. I thought I was going to lose her, too."

"It won't take me long to fix this." He gathered Dolly in his arms, but turned to look back at Monica from the door. "Look, you seem upset. Would you like to go for a coffee once Dolly is settled? There's a coffee-house right around the corner."

"I...sure." Monica lifted her head and smiled. "Thank you for asking. At least I know now why you didn't think I was crazy with my 'goose talk' at the cemetery. You're a vet! "

"I thought you were a lovely woman, kind and caring. I..." he paused. "I almost asked you out. But.."

"Why didn't you?" Monica asked curiously.

"I thought you were married. Your ring," and he nodded at her hand, "and your son and all."

"Divorced. We broke up right after Mark's death. But it's been five years, five long years..and I'd love to go for coffee."

As she reached out a hand, Dr. John Carpenter reached out in return. He clasped her fingers before turning to Dolly.

A satisfied almost smug, "Honk, honk," sounded from the examining table.

"Goose talk," Monica grinned, "and I need a translation. Dolly, what do you mean?"

Dr. John Carpenter peered at the bird. "I think she's trying to tell us she's a matchmaker in disguise. And she's just made her match for the day!"

And he looked at Monica and smiled.

Author Bio

Please see Linda Lehmann Masek's Bio on page 122 of this Anthology.

A Special Boy's Fantasy On
Easter
by
Pamela Saraga

Keenen was a special boy. He loved to run deep into the woods and climb trees. He could talk to animals. He knew what they were thinking. His Mother worried that he spent too much time alone. How could she know he was never alone, because in his mind lived many people?

He would usually run into the forest with Billy. Billy was a fast runner and would fly by Keenen like he was standing still. He would run so fast that he would disappear into the forest and run back into Keenen's mind.

Rupert liked to climb trees. They would scramble up a pine tree like two squirrels then they would perch on a tall branch. They would talk about the day or make plans about tomorrow. Rupert was almost Keenen's best friend. But his really best friend was Mable. She was kind and understanding. She never tried to beat him at sports or argue about school projects. They talked about important stuff. Where his dad had gone? Why Joe Butler tried to hit him all the time? Why the kids at school never wanted to sit with him at lunch?

Keenen loved Sunday, especially Easter Sunday. His mom would dress up and put on a silly hat. She would put him in a special suit with a real tie and dark shoes that shinned like glass. They would walk the three blocks down the tree lined lane and go in the old wooden church. There were always lots of people, but on Easter the building overflowed with people and music. Mrs. Bishop would play the large organ and every one would sing. He would be filled up with the music and feel like he belonged. And on Easter there were always lots of cakes.

On this particular Sunday, Mabel just showed up. She was there sitting two rows down from him. Everyone could see her, and they gave her cake and she sang along with the choir in a strong, sweet voice. He had never seen her outside the forest. But there she was. The congregation moved to the recreation hall for the feast. When he was able to go over to her and find out how she had managed to escape from his mind, she told him she was lonely too and wanted to see all the people at the church. She smiled and told him the cake was too delicious not to taste it with her own mouth.

Keenen's Mother looked over at her son talking to the little girl. She was so happy that he had finally found a friend. The two kids sat close together talking and eating. They smiled and held hands. It was nice to be with Mable, this way, face to face. He closed his eyes and thought about Billy and Rupert. Whoosh, Billy ran past him straight for the food then Rupert pushed past him moving toward the front of the hall. It was a great day.

Suddenly, the back of the room grew silent. The entire group moved back taking one step after another. Slowly pausing in wonder at the sight, there standing alone in the doorway was a man with the light of the early afternoon sun streaming in behind him. He had on a black tuxedo with a white flower stuck, crookedly in his lapel.

Slowly a murmur began again which grew into a moving mass as everyone in the back, moved toward the front of the room and away from the door. The look of fear, the smell of fear, filled the area. The congregation recognized the man in the suit. He was young Keenen's father.

He had worn that suit only two times before, once at his wedding and then again at his funeral. There, left standing alone stood the man. He looked around the room; and when he saw Keenen, he strode quickly toward him.

Keenen looked up just in time to see his mother scream and run between him and the man. She held out her hands, shaking like she was possessed. He looked carefully at the stranger. The black tux with the white flower and the smile looked just like the picture on his nightstand. This was what he wanted, a mom and a dad, friends and music.

Why was everybody acting so weird? As the man grew closer, everyone could see he was not a whole man. His back was oddly flat with a black felt material covering it. A cardboard stand jutted out of his spine which dragged along behind. He was just like the picture. That was all the boy knew of him, a picture on a nightstand.

His mother looked at Keenen.

"Send him away boy. He doesn't belong here!"

His father wavered like a mirage on a hot day, and then slowly vanished into the air, leaving only a whisper of a breeze.

He hadn't been told that his father died in a car crash three days before he was born.

It was Easter, a time for resurrections, and Keenen was a very special boy.

Author Bio:

Raised by wolverines, less social than wolves and a lot more vicious, I am a mother, a veteran and a social cripple. What else could I do after retiring from 37 years of suppressed creativity and boredom as a postal worker, but become a writer? The work has enhanced my imagination so that most of my short stories have a surprise ending in subjects ranging from the funny to the macabre. Most of the stories are from my life experiences except for those ending in murder; those are only wishful thinking.

Originally from New York which explains some of the residual hostility, I have lived in Northern California for 42 years. My only real experience writing has been for the Mercury Register, our local newspaper. I won the North State Voices column and wrote for a year. I am also a proud member of *Write On Writers Group* in Oroville.

I self-published my first novel, *Amazon Diet,* a comic adventure about several over-weight women who take a vacation in Suriname to have fun and lose some weight. Their journey back to civilization makes them realize that they didn't need a trip into the Amazon to improve themselves. They are perfect just the way they are. It's a fun read with a message about body image, and is available at most all outlets in paperback and eBook form.

Have You Hugged A Tree Today?
by
Joan West

It's Arbor Day! Have you hugged a tree today? We have a beauty in front of our house – a Drake elm ... a beauty in the fullness of summer and a bare-limbed skeleton in winter. And, how does it come to the skeleton-like condition? Sometime in mid-October, it begins to undress. In its hurry, it doesn't just drop leaves, it drops bits of branches covered with leaves and, hurry though it does, Grandfather Drake doesn't complete the task until sometime about mid-February.

My husband, Glen, and I spend hours of back-breaking labor sweeping the leaves into piles and putting the piles into big sturdy paper leaf bags from the hardware store. And when I say *back-breaking*, I mean that literally as it takes an equal number of hours for us to straighten up when finished – well, not exactly *finished* – *finished* doesn't happen until every last leaf has released itself from the tree, sometime around *Valentine's Day*.

Now you might think that rather than hug our tree, we might be inclined to want to kick it. Not so. Glen can even be heard to mummer sweet nothings into its distinctive red bark ... bark, which incidentally, flakes off in great pieces along with its leaves.

And that brings up an interesting question. Glen's birthday is on *Valentine's Day*. Do you suppose that last leaf drifting down on a gentle February breeze is the tree's birthday present to the one who watches over it so faithfully?

Now I'm really waxing poetic off the deep end, am I not?

Maybe yes; maybe no. How different from birthday wishes from a tree is Prince Charles' talking to his plants? Speaking of his garden, the prince, has said, "I just come and talk to the plants, really – very important to talk to them; they respond."

And Charles is not alone. Many gardeners talk to their plants and much research has been collected on the subject. Sciencenet suggests that "plants need carbon dioxide to grow, and when you talk to a plant, you breathe on it, giving it an extra infusion of CO_2." Lest you think talking to plants is a new or isolated idea, think again. Way back in

1848, German professor, Dr. Gustav Theodor Fechner thought that plants, like humans, have emotions. That being the case, they would respond to attention, including talk, by growing big and healthy. Dr. Fechner is joined by no less a plant person than botanist Luther Burbank, who believed that while plants might not understand the spoken word, they telepathically could understand the meaning of speech.

Further, our leafed – or would it be leaved? – friends respond to music. More than one study, confirms the belief that soothing music, think classical, is beneficial to plants. On the other hand, "loud aggressive music"—read: rock music – causes plants "to wither and die." Who would have thought!

But, before you scoff, scientists have narrowed some of this information down to specifics. Studies have found responses in two plant genes: rbcS and Ald; whatever they are. And injured tomato plants *talk* to other plants, who respond by releasing chemicals to deter insect predators. So, who's to say?

Not content with one tree in our front yard, Glen offered a contribution to the Arbor Day Foundation and, in return, they sent him a crape myrtle tree. Well, what they actually sent is a small stick with hairs on one end.

It reminds me of the peach tree I sent to my mother a few years ago. My mother, unlike her daughter, had a green thumb. In her back yard in Clearwater, Florida, she grew grapefruit and oranges and limes; but she wasn't satisfied. She wanted a peach tree. Now, Florida is not known for its peach trees, but what my mother wanted, my mother got and I, living in Georgia at the time, was assigned to the "getting."

I took the easy way out – I thought – and ordered one from a mail order catalogue.

The *tree* was delivered the day before I arrived for a weekend visit. She took me into the garage, lifted up a stick, looking much like Glen's crape myrtle, and said, "You call this a tree?"

Back to the drawing board! Returning to Georgia, I went to a local nursery and purchased a fine looking young tree about five feet tall. I was teaching at a college and this was on a Tuesday afternoon. I planned to go down to Clearwater on Friday right after my last class; so, I stood the tree, still in its pot, into the middle of my front flower border. Something, I don't remember what, came up, and I wasn't able to go to Florida for another couple of weeks. At the appointed time, I started to lift the pot holding the tree into my car. It wouldn't budge. The peach tree had taken root in my border. Afraid that I would break the roots and kill it, if I insisted, I made a quick stop at the nursery on my way out of town and bought another peach tree for my mother.

Florida or not, she had it bearing Georgia peaches in no time.

But back to Glen's crape myrtle: the day after it arrived, he came into the kitchen looking at the brochure that had accompanied it.

"You need to plant the tree before it dies," he said.

"You? Did you say *you*, as in *me*?"

"Well, yes, you're the gardener in the family."

Now, let me stop right here and straighten that out. A gardener, I'm not. I'd like to be. I have at least a half dozen garden books on my book shelves, and I subscribe to garden magazines, and I planted a garden outside our screen room this summer; however, by last count, I've lost half of the plants I put in, including a lovely gardenia bush. Thank goodness, the camellia seems to be thriving. It's still small, but loaded with beautiful red blossoms.

But, I digress.

"I may be the one who plants the plants, but I'm not a *gardener* and especially not in the winter time. It's cold out there," I told him.

"Well, it says here that if you can't plant it right away, you should dig a trench…"

"Stop with the trenches! Just leave everything and I'll see what I can do."

Did I mention that another tree is the last thing we need in our yard? A little more grass, a few less weeds, but not another tree to join the magnolias, the huge drake elm and the towering live oaks.

Bottom line: I found a large round bare spot onto which the sun happened to be shinning, dug a hole, used lots of water, as directed by the brochure, put in the stick, hairs down, and added mulch. Good luck, little tree.

But, no matter what, we sweep on, gathering leaves and whispering to Grandfather Drake.

Happy Arbor Day to you and your trees. Humor me and go outside and hug one.

Author Bio:

Following a career as a college professor, Joan West was a founding partner in the Bennett & West Literary Agency. Later, along with her partner, Lois Bennett, she founded Fireside Publications. Now retired, she devotes herself to writing, gardening, and enjoying life in Central Florida with husband Glen. Her most recent work is *Disappearing Daisies: An Ellen Kerry Mystery*.

*Seeking Independence and a Better Life in America, the Wells Family
Found a*

Happy Christmas – 1947

by
Julie Clark

This is a true story of an English family's immigration to the United States in December, 1947. The Wells family all originated in the Greater London area and had endured the bombing inflicted on London throughout World War II.

Our family home was in Surrey. Providing for a family at that time was difficult and costly, even for the educated and employed. Even today, Surrey still has the highest cost of living in England, outside of London itself. My father had a degree as a Chemist. With his degree, he was fortunate to have been able to work as a research paint chemist in Kingston-on-Thames, for twenty years. He was then able to obtain employment in the United States after the war. We would be living in Louisville, Kentucky.

The Wells Family

We journeyed to Louisville in December of 1947, arriving shortly before the Christmas holidays. We traveled first on the *Aquitania* to Halifax, Nova Scotia in Canada. From there, we traveled through the frozen North where the St. Lawrence River was solid ice. It was a sight to behold, especially for a 12-year-old youngster.

We continued on, and eventually passed through Detroit, Michigan. We then changed accommodations and took a train to Louisville, Kentucky, the Gateway to the South. This circuitous route became necessary and took place because the **DeGrasse** ship's company, in which we had been scheduled to sail Southampton to New York as first class passengers, had gone out on strike in France.

Mostly my personal memories of this journey are very few; my Dad, I do remember, was very stressed initially by trying to get our big trunk on board the train. In Canada, the train was much overheated; and they didn't allow the windows to be opened. We were able to see a lot of the Canadian countryside and glimpse some of its bigger cities because we had stops in Toronto and in Montreal. Perhaps my most vivid memory of Canada was from Montreal, where Bing Crosby's song *White Christmas* played endlessly. The words of the song, I recall, were quite appropriate to our surroundings at that time..

I, the oldest of the children, was born in 1935. There were two younger siblings, both of whom are still living. The three of us were awestruck and thrilled to see the endless wonders that continually unfolded before our eyes until we finally reached Louisville, Kentucky.

A Dodge car was waiting for my Dad upon his arrival. The wartime problems were quickly forgotten. We no longer had to shield our presence behind blackout curtains; V1 and V2 raids and casualties in the neighborhood were no longer an everyday occurrence.

The Wells' family's English relatives and friends gathered for a send-off party for us in Surbiton in 1949. But our contacts with them gradually diminished over the years. The last time I was to see any of my relatives still living in London was in 1958, when I was married to a military man and working in Holland.

The Louisville people were warm and welcoming. I was able to tell them a little about our life in England at Southern Junior High School. I was a novelty at that time since not too many immigrant families settle in Kentucky. Now, I live in California where over 25% of the population is foreign born.

My parents retired to Clearwater, Florida and lived into old age. My brother has also lived in California a long time; and my sister's family is well traveled and resides in Vermont. Our lives were so completely changed by uprooting from England and becoming integrated into an American lifestyle. The initial change was so extreme that my mother used to go to the supermarket just to look at all the food.

Immigration's impact in the United States has been enormous. What would it have been like for us in 1847? The waves of immigration have changed over the years immensely. Coal-mining, steel-producing, railroads, gold and silver mining, textiles have all benefitted from the various ethnic groups. Immigration is a well documented subject and there have been enormous changes of course since 1847, 1947, until now. It has always meant the land of opportunity to the foreign born, for us and continues to be for millions. Every day has been a new adventure - a true gift, indeed.

Author Bio:

Julie Clark was born in Surbiton, Surrey, England which is now Greater London. She grew up during World War II, and with her English family of five emigrated to Louisville, Kentucky in 1947. She became a U.S. citizen in the 1950's. She graduated high school in Dayton Ohio in 1952 then Miami-Jacobs Business School and worked as a legal secretary all her life. She lived and worked at various locations around the country and abroad while married, eventually settling in California. Julie is widowed and lives in rural northern California. For the past two years, she has been a member of the Write-On group as well as completing volunteer patrols for several years with the Sheriff's Team of Active Retired Seniors (STARS).

July 4th - 1971
Near Death in The Gila

by
Don Lubov

So this is the way it ends – lying by the side of an old logging road, waiting to die. What a waste! To go from a life of unbridled hedonism...rather appropriate for a single guy, to getting a wake-up call to what life is really all about, just in time to have to cozy up to death.

Camping here in the Gila has been a real eye-opener... 3.3 million acres of rugged terrain – Geronimo country. I love the awesome cliff dwellings from six-hundred years ago and beautiful sunrises and sunsets. How these people survived out here, way back when, is a mystery to me. Each day is a struggle just to stay alive. I've never been so physically exhausted and yet, so spiritually alive. Four thousand miles of hot, dusty, backpacking – a seven-day, outdoor rock festival in the woods, an invitation to a lynching, a close encounter with Mexican drug dealers, months of triple-digit heat by day and freezing at night and a life-changing awakening from God.

It certainly hasn't been boring. Now I know, down to my bones, that I'm part of some-thing greater than myself. What am I to do with this magnificent new mindset? What good can come from this knowledge if I can't get out of this place? I'm probably going to die...this day, this hour, right here, right now.
Within a few days there won't even be any remains – What the bears don't get the mountain lions will. I'll be dust before anyone knows I'm missing. What the heck is it all for? Thirty years of hard work and playing around and for what?...to die alone, in the high desert country – out of food, out of water, lost and worn out. With this enlightenment I can accept my mortality, my death. But, why now? Why so soon after discovering the ultimate treasure?

Now that I have a purpose in my life; now that my life has meaning – I can help others make some sense out of their lives. Now that I know what it means to be a human being what happens? – I'm being groomed for the main course at the roadkill café. My parents will never know what happened to me. I've been too busy, too much on the move…like a cork in a swift moving stream..just bobbing along, aimlessly. And now, I won't have a wife or kids either. Nothing will be left to pass on and no one to pass it on to. What a shame. I have so much to offer, now.

It all seems rather pointless. I mean, you know – you listen to your parents, go to school, get a career – In my case teaching art on the university level. Have a little fun…OK, a lot of fun. Live a non-threatening life-style and BAM, you're predator lunchmeat. I never dreamed I'd end up like this. How could I? What's a city boy doing way out here, in the wilderness, by himself, with a backpack? What ever possessed me to think that going on-the-road at age 29 was the right thing to do? How could I be so stupid? What do I know about camping? I don't even have a decent sense of direction.

No one to share my epiphany with. No one to help with their awakening. No books to write. No lectures to give. Lessons learned but not to be passed on…all too briefly. From what's it all about? Is this all there is? To Aha! I get it, To, I'm screwed. All in thirty years.

Well, so be it. Out of food, out of water and too tired to stand. Physically lost but spiritually found. I'm coming home. Back to where I started, only now I know what it means to be here now…in the moment. So long outside. Hello inside. Getting weaker. Giving in to that long, long sleep. Shutting down. Goodbye all.

What's that? I heard a sound – an unnatural sound – a mechanical sound. Well, son-of-a-gun…a truck – out here, in the middle of nowhere. If I can just get to my feet I know he'll see me. I'll just stand here in the middle of the road. He'll have to stop then…or run me over.

Yes! Yes! He's slowing down. If I wasn't so dehydrated, I'd cry tears of joy. I DO get a second chance. I DO get to share. This is NOT my time to die. On the contrary, it's my time to really live…for the first time. Thank you! Thank you!

Even now, 40 years after this life-altering event, I get shivers just thinking about what happened in the summer of 1971. I've never felt alone since this incident; never doubted its authenticity. Things happen when and where they are supposed to happen. There are no coincidences.

Happy Independence Day

Author Bio:

Don Lubov has held membership in FWA - 2006-2013, and in Writers Bloc at Del Webb Spruce Creek CC from 2006 to the present. He writes for or has previously written for: Yahoo, Beliefnet.com and Kinja.com. Multi-talented, Don has self-published eight books and taught art/design for eight years on the university level. Currently he teach courses in spirituality at Del Webb, The Villages Lifelong Learning College and MTP College at On Top Of the World. He has three YouTube videos: "The Grassroots Manifesto - Malthus Was Wrong, "The Spirituality Manifesto" and "Creativity Manifesto". From 1966 - 2005, Don worked as a full-time artist.

Please see: donlubov.com and Spiritshare.net. Email: lubov11971@yahoo.com

Part Four

Halloween

Mysteries of the Night

Visit the Spooky Land
of Truths and Half-truths

Dancing Across the Veil
by
Carla Lee Suson

"Wow, Layne! If you go trick-or-treating in that, you may get more than you bargained for!" The ghost's voice cut through the air as I walked into the living room.

"Thanks Charles. The Northwest Indiana Paranormal group's hosting an old-fashioned masquerade. What do you think?" I put on the fancy peacock blue mask and struck a pose in the matching ball gown.

"Too delicious for that crowd. Why are you bothering?"

I sighed, pulling off the mask.

"I'm hoping to develop friendships with people who breathe. Most folks are freaked out by my ability to work with the dead. The NWIP folks already know I'm spirit-talker so maybe they'll be different."

"Freaked out?"

I forgot the hundred-year-old spirit didn't always keep up on modern slang.

"Bothered, worried... in some cases, terrified." I waved a hand. "Even the guys I've dated react like I'm either crazy or evil. In truth, I'm lonely most of the time."

"Hmph. I keep forgetting that none of them can talk to ghosts."

"Yeah, I'm the only one. Most of the investigators from the group have dealt with some kind of haunting and some have seen me in action. We don't get time to socialize while we work so I'm hoping tonight will be different."

"If I was still alive and saw you in that dress, you wouldn't make it to the ball."

I smiled while checking the contents of my clutch. My friend for ten years was a passionate man from the 1920s who loved all the vices of his generation. Even in his dead status, he was still a lecher.

"If you were alive, you wouldn't even notice me."

"You're wrong, Ducky. You're so very wro..."

The voice faded away as Charles used up the rest of his energy. Without obtaining warmth from the fireplace or energy from batteries,

145

he could not gain enough power for speech or an appearance without resting for hours.

"I'll see you later," I replied as I headed out the door.

With wine glass in hand, I watched the people mingle in the banquet hall, all bedecked in formal attire along with feather and sequin filled masks. Those arriving without a cover were encouraged to choose from a selection near the door. However, the highly decorated masks only covered the upper part of the face so they failed to hide anyone's identity.

Doubt and insecurity again began to fill my mind. Other than the spirits, I never had many friends. A few people acknowledged me with a wave or a nod but no one made any further efforts of socialization. Coming here may have been a mistake.

"You look kinda lost." I jumped a little at the deep voice from behind me. The alcohol mist jumped across the space between us as Burt Sorenson, the President of the group, faced me and grinned. He leaned in and winked. "It's me, by the way." His black and white disguise featured a checkerboard pattern that matched the white dinner jacket and the graying touches in his beard.

"Hi, Burt. This ball was a great idea."

"Thanks. Did you buy your silent auction tickets?"

I nodded, flashing the twenty dollars worth of colored paper in my hand. The prizes along with their donation jars decorated a long table on one side of the room and included gift certificates for local eateries, free Chicago tours, and ghost hunting equipment such as a handheld tape recorder, camcorder, and a spirit box. The last item sounded impressive but was in fact a refitted radio that constantly changed frequencies in search of beyond-the-grave voices.

"I'll probably stick with the gift certificates. I don't usually use most of that equipment."

"Yep, not like you need a spirit box to hear the ghosts, right?" The big man chuckled. "Rick Master's mom donated most of the paranormal stuff. We're going to give half the proceeds back to her. Even though it was six months ago, she's still paying off his debts."

"I'm so sorry to hear about his accident."

Burt nodded, looking somber. "Yeah, I miss him a lot. Folks say that he was drunk, but I don't believe it. I saw a picture of the car, you know, afterwards. The semi trailer sheared off the top." He downed the last of his wine and beamed at me in a visible effort to lighten the mood. "Did you bring a date?"

"No."

"Then why aren't you mingling?"

I shrugged.

"Everyone seems to be pairing off. You know that I have trouble approaching folks I don't know."

He slipped an arm around my shoulders. "Come on. I'll help you out."

As we drew near to a small group of four women, the DJ started the evening's music off with Michael Jackson's *Thriller*. Three couples took to the dance floor, forming up a line for their zombie moves.

The women's talk trailed off, and they shot us wary glances as we got closer. Burt smiled, providing an air of good humor.

"Evening, ladies. You look lovely tonight. Tina, Cheryl, you know Layne Knowles, right?"

Tina flipped back a blond curl and gave me a curt nod, while Cheryl avoided eye contact.

Burt continued. "If I'm not mistaken, this vision in white is Megan and those pink feathers hide the pretty face of Jennifer. Did you all buy tickets for the silent auction? We have some great stuff tonight."

The women nodded, displaying tickets and smiling at the man's cheer.

"Layne's feeling a bit lonely. Can you help her out?" He waved at someone across the room, and strolled off before they could answer.

The seconds ticked by in discomfort as we flashed faux smiles at each other and I searched for anything to say.

Jennifer broke the silence first.

"So you're the one, right?"

"Uhm, I'm not sure what you mean." I replied.

"Yeah, she's the medium." Tina swallowed a mouthful of red wine before continuing. "I told Jenny and Meg about the Mackenzie house investigation last month." She paused for a moment, and then rushed ahead. "What I don't understand is why you're never afraid."

"What happened?" Megan asked, turning to me.

Tina answered instead. "Things really got weird that night. The spook had scratched people and thrown things. But you just walked in and started chewing it out like you were its mother. I don't get that."

"Actually, I didn't really chew Agnes out. I simply asked her to be nicer so we could help her out." I replied quietly.

"Agnes?"

"Yes, you kept calling the spirit an 'it,' but her name was Agnes."

"How do you do it?" Jennifer asked, and a faint fluster of redness appeared under her feathered mask. "I mean, we all try to engage the ghosts, but often they only respond to you. And they appear in front of you. That doesn't happen to anyone else."

I grew still, trying to think of some way of explaining how my special ability worked, the same talent that made so many people afraid of me.

"I'm just really sensitive to hearing the dead. However, you get better results when you treat them more like regular people. Don't go in asking a lot of pointed questions. Introduce yourself. Be polite. I know that Jared, Mike, and some of the others like to engage the spirits by cussing them out or making them angry, but that doesn't really work. After all, if some guy started yelling at you, would you bother answering or would you simply leave?"

The women exchanged looks and shifted around a bit as the music switched to the *Monster Mash*. Tina put on a smile that reeked of false cheer and spoke.

"Hey, I haven't heard this in years. I'm going to see if Tony wants to dance. See you later."

She slipped off, and the others fell into another uncomfortable silence as we watched people gyrate to the old tune.

I tried a different tack, turning towards Megan.

"Have you been with NWIP for long?"

"About four years. I joined at the same time as Cheryl." The redhead next to her nodded in agreement. "But I don't have a lot of time now for the investigations. How about you?"

"About six months."

Cheryl giggled a little and put a hand to her mouth for a moment. "Sorry. I just remembered your training video, Layne."

I dropped my eyes, feeling equal parts embarrassment and sadness rise up. That horrible short film was the reason most people declined to team up with me during an investigation.

"What happened?" Megan asked.

"Well, Marty was supposed to put the new trainees through a test, right? You remember that tech guy who always liked to show off." Cheryl said.

Megan nodded, giving me an odd look.

"He took Layne in and acted like this big tough guy, cussing out the spook. Once her turn came, Layne simply called out to the ghost. A Civil War soldier appeared right in front of them. Marty shot out the door in an absolute panic. He pretty much did everything we're taught not to do. Remember, Layne?"

"Uhm, yeah." I mumbled, staring hard into my empty wine glass.

Megan nodded.

"I haven't seen him for a while though."

"He quit after that." Jennifer added in a quiet monotone. "He said he didn't like the new types of people we started accepting into the group."

I bit my lip and tried to think of some polite way of excusing myself when Megan spoke up. "Hey, who's that?" She gestured at a newcomer. A tall, handsome man in a midnight-colored mask sauntered across the room, pausing for a moment to watch the dancers writhing to *Devil Went Down to Georgia*.

"I don't know, but I'd love to run my hands through those dark curls."

Jennifer stretched up on tiptoes to get a better view.

The man's old-fashioned tuxedo, complete with short coat and tails, stood in stark contrast against the more modern apparel in the room. However, the antique Hollywood movie attire accentuated his well-built frame and long legs. Eventually, his focus came to rest on our small group.

Cheryl gave a small gasp as he strolled towards us, stopping a short distance away. With one white-gloved hand pressed against his abdomen, he bowed deeply and made a grand flourish with the other hand. After unfolding, he reached towards us with one hand palm up.

As the one closest to him, Megan tittered a little and placed her hand on his. With a seductive smile, he lowered his head to kiss the back of her hand. He shifted next to Megan and then Jennifer, executing the same courtly behavior.

When he reached out for me, I hesitated. His manners seemed unreal, like an elaborate joke. However, I felt like I was falling into his silver gray eyes, transfixed by the intensity of his stare. He tilted his head to one side, giving me a broader smile and nod of encouragement. When I finally touched his hand, he gently pulled me closer. With tenderness, he lifted my hand and kissed the palm, sending shivers down my back. Stepping to my side, he placed my arm around his elbow and began drawing me away from the others. I glanced back at the girls feeling confused, and saw the same look echoed back with a small mix of jealousy thrown in.

He led me to the dance floor and struck a pose, waiting for me to join in. The music had switched to Nat King Cole's *Unforgettable*, making many of the earlier rock and roll enthusiasts surrender the area to more committed couples.

I stepped closer. With one firm arm around my waist, he drew me in and took my hand in his. I felt the solid muscles through the suit. Feeling a little unsettled, my head came to rest against his chest as we began to move. His touch felt cold even through the gloves and the smell of cigarette smoke tugged at my memory. A name filled my mind, impossible to believe and yet hard to ignore. We swayed in unspoken peace for a few moments before I whispered, "Charles?"

"Can't fool you, Ducky." He leaned back a bit so I could see the wide grin and bawdy wink.

My jaw dropped in amazement.

"How...?"

"Hmm," He stepped back, pulling my arm upward so that I would twirl away and then back against him. "To start with, it is the beginning of the Days of the Dead, Samhain, or Halloween, whatever you want to call it. Turns out that the old religions got it right. The veil between the living and the dead really is at its thinnest tonight." Another twirl and we flowed into a dip as the song ended.

As *Moon River* started, he pulled me upright and we started moving again in a waltz. Others left the dance floor, leaving only us and two other couples. "Luckily the music master's collection featured some decent selections. I requested these oldies just for us." He beamed down at me.

"Where did you get the clothes?"

"You often point out that we control the shape our energy takes. Do you really think I don't remember any of the hundreds of times I've worn a tuxedo in my spoiled and misspent youth?"

"The mask?"

"I picked up one at the door."

He twirled me slowly again before continuing.

"The other factor involves the amount of energy I'm using to stay solid for you. I'll explain that mystery by saying you now have a cabinet filled with dead batteries."

I pulled back a little to look up at his face.

"That supply was to last for months in dealing with the spooks. Why, Charles?"

"To have the chance to hold you in my arms for one night" he said. We stopped, and he gently lifted my mask off, smoothing my long brown hair back down again. "Don't send me away, Ducks. Give me this one night." His gray eyes bore into me, waiting for an answer.

Realizing people were watching, I took his hand again and we resumed our slow progress in rhythm.

"Show me your face." I whispered.

"Why?"

"You hardly appear in body form anymore. It's hard to remember what you look like."

With one hand, he tugged the cloth and sequin-covered plastic off. My best friend for the last ten years smiled down at me. The high cheekbones fitted in with a slender aquiline nose and wide lips that seem to twitch with amusement.

"You're staring." He murmured.

I dropped my eyes and then chuckled.

"So what's next?"

"Nothing, Ducky, except for me to be your companion tonight. Consider this my Valentine's gift to you, just four months early. Tomorrow my energy will be diminished and everything will return to the way it always is."

I smiled as we finished the dance.

"Sounds great."

Throughout the evening, he took up the role of the silent suitor again whenever anyone else was around. Disappearing at odd moments, he always returned a few minutes later, with a drink or a small plate of food in hand for me. Some of the ladies vied for his attention but he simply put them off with a small bow and a hand on his heart. As each love song came on, he gently pulled me back to the dance floor and his cool embrace.

As the clock moved towards eleven, Burt announced the silent auction was closing, encouraging everyone to purchase more tickets. The DJ started Little River Band's *Cool Change,* and I leaned into Charles's arms one more time.

"Charles, thank you for tonight. I was feeling pretty worthless until you showed up. Folks here aren't interested in friendship either."

"Their loss, Ducks. If I were alive, you'd never feel alone again."
He lowered his head until his lips touched the edge of my cheek. "I've
said this to very few women in my life." His grip tightened around my
waist.

"Layne, I lo-"

Discordant music and voices exploded out of the spirit box's
speakers, making people jump and cry out in pain. Charles's arms fell
away as I rocked back, putting my hands to my ears. Then Jennifer
shrieked, drawing everyone's attention to the auction table. The EMF
meter came alive, ticking madly while the K2 boxes' lights flared off
and on, pegging out at the maximum range.

Charles gripped my hand tightly and moved to block me from the
table.

The volume on the spirit box lowered to a lesser roar. The noise
turned into words coming through first in a stuttering racket and then
more clearly into one male voice in pain.

"Layne... Ca... can... hear me?"

Jennifer turned pale and staggered back from the table. "Oh my
God, that's Rick's voice."

A din of frantic talking rose as some panicked and backed from
the electronics, while others pulled out cell phones, pointing the
cameras at the table.

Burt shouted above the commotion. "Calm down!"

As the crowd settled, he took one step towards the machine.

"Rick, is that you?"

The young man's voice rose again through the buzzing, clearer
this time.

"Layne... you there?"

Like marionettes on the same strings, the crowd turned to look at
me, and the angry whispers began.

"Layne, please... help me."

Charles and I stepped towards the small, black box.

"I'm here." I said loudly. "I can hear you, Rick."

The voice started with a sob.

"Of anyone ... I knew... need help."

I looked at Charles whose eyes filled with sadness. My heart
broke to see him looking so lost. With lips pressed together, he nodded
as we shared the same thoughts. I could not leave the spirit in pain, but
our night, our only time to hold each other, was over. I released his hand
and stepped towards the speaker.

152

"What do you need me to do?" I said loud enough to carry across the frightened chattering.

The words broke up with static. "Tell my mom... Tell her, I'm sorry.... The brakes failed..., wasn't drinking."

"I'll tell her. I promise."

"So cold here.... I'm scared."

I closed my eyes and took a deep breath. Like many who suddenly died, the spirit did not move on to the beyond. If I were alone, I could help him open up the doorway and cross over to the next dimension; but the siren call of that place pulled at living souls as well, endangering those who could not resist its alluring beauty. A cleansing was unthinkable in a hall filled with half-drunk revelers.

A collective gasp cut through the air behind me. I whirled in time to see Charles' mask falling to the floor as he faded away. A soft touch stroked my cheeks. "Don't worry, Layne. I'll help him."

"Take him to the house, and we'll show him the way tonight," I said to my old friend.

I moved towards Burt, who took an involuntary step back before stopping himself.

"I'll need you to give me his mom's address."

The big man nodded, his pale face wet with tears. "When you are ready, call me and we'll go together."

I nodded, and turned to collect my coat. A pathway parted in front as people shifted away to keep their distance. However, the remarks borne from their fear flowed all around.

"I touched him..."

"...Some kind of freak."

"It's just wrong..."

"... make them go away."

I left with my head held high, but my heart filled with pain. Some of the participants fled to the parking lot as well, walking to their cars in controlled haste. Stopping by the hood of my old Jeep, I felt the night breeze flowing through my hair and drying my tears. I did the right thing in helping the dead, but it always cost me any chance of friendship. It was no wonder that spirit-talkers often took their own lives.

Instead of car engines roaring to life in the darkness, the sound of clicking and frustrated door slams filled the air. A male voice shouted at others in the parking lot.

"Hey, can anyone give me a jump? My car won't start."

"Mine either!" Another called out.

Several other voices rose in anger with the same complaint.

"Is anyone's car working?" Megan yelled from her blue Volkswagen.

Fighting to hide a smile, I whispered. "Charles, what did you do?"

The words came across the air. "Don't worry, Ducky. I left your car alone, but I needed to get more power from somewhere to stay solid. Happy Halloween."

The last syllables faded away as the old spook departed.

I got into my Wrangler, and the engine turned over without hesitation. Pausing for a moment, I whispered, "I love you too Charles," before putting the car into gear to help those who needed it.

Author Bio:

Carla Lee Suson started writing after working in molecular and cellular biology research. She took up the pen while raising her three kids and a passel of dogs in the Coastal Bend area of Texas. She spent ten years developing short stories, articles, and standardized test materials. Her topics included travel articles, parenting advice, children's stories, and science work. In addition, she also collaborated with local experts in editing their books in art, art history, climatology, and water rights. After moving to Northwest Indiana, she obtained a Master's degree in Professional Writing and published her first book, *Independence Day Plague*. When not sculpting tales of ghosts, murder, and mayhem, she dives into one of her many hobbies such as woodworking, leather craft, and quilting. *Independence Day Plague* is still available on Amazon/Kindle and on the Publisher's website at www.firepubs.com .

Halloween Happenings in the Midwest
by
Linda Lehmann Masek

The movie, *The Shawshank Redemption*, is about hope and despair, friendship and love, and has been ranked as one of the five best movies of all time. Viewers report seeing it as many as fifty times. There is a very intimate connection between this classic box office phenomenon and Ohio.

The "Shawshank Redemption" was filmed almost entirely at the Ohio State Reformatory at Mansfield, which is celebrating the 20-year anniversary since the film was released. The film starring Morgan Freeman and Tim Robbins probes the psychology of the friendship of two men, locked away in the bowels of the earth, a prison from which they likely will never see the light of day. Although the site of this film has been closed as a prison for decades, the reformatory has had a rebirth as a location for numerous films.

The Ohio State Reformatory, with its Gothic architecture, has served as a movie set for three other films, including *Air Force One*, with Harrison Ford; *Tango & Cash* with Sylvester Stallone; and *Harry & Walter Go to New York* with James Caan; plus a series of music videos. The building has had a long and colorful history; originally the site was a Civil War soldier training camp. When first erected, the Mansfield building was meant to house young boys who were possible rehabilitation subjects rather than sending these early offenders to the Columbus Penitentiary.

The architect of the building, which has been referred to as a Draculean structure, was Levi T. Scofield from Cleveland, Ohio. It was originally meant to resemble a cathedral so young offenders would be encouraged to reform their ways and be better citizens.

The people of Mansfield's business and political communities welcomed the reformatory. There was an extensive ceremony when the cornerstone was first laid in 1886. It was considered *Mansfield's Greatest Day* by the population, and the city raised $10,000 to buy the 30 acres needed plus 150 extra acres for an additional $20,000. The 15,000 people who turned out for the ceremonies were not disappointed;

these included speeches by Rutherford B. Hayes, former U.S. President, Senator John Sherman, the governor and several others.

Because of monetary problems, it was ten years later before the reformatory finally opened. When the prisoners arrived from Columbus, they were met by festive crowds along the route. Cigars were even passed out to the prisoners, who seemed in high spirits. Local newspapers talked about the prisoners as though they were famous celebrities.

The Ohio State Reformatory was completed in 1896; the earliest inmates were occupied with helping to erect a 25 foot wall around the prison and building a sewer system inside.

The prison has been home to a few *celebrities* over the years; Kevin Mack, running back, spent a month in jail there before returning to the Cleveland Browns football team; Henry Baker of the Brinks Gang also was incarcerated here as was baseball player Gates Brown of the Detroit Tigers.

As with all institutions of this kind, the Ohio State Reformatory has had its share of prison disasters. Two corrections officers were killed. There was also the episode of the *Mad Dog Killers*, Robert Daniels and John West. In 1948, the pair killed Earl Ambrose who owned a Columbus tavern before driving to Mansfield in a stolen vehicle. The two then kidnapped and killed the John Niebel family before committing another murder in Tiffin. The criminals were captured in Van Wert, Ohio. West was killed; Daniels died in the electric chair the following year thus ending the saga of the most famous of criminals from the institution.

The prison officially closed in December, 1990; the prisoners were housed elsewhere. Aside from the movies which were shot on location in this actual reformatory, the site has gotten a reputation for spirits which haunt the premises, especially on dark and starless nights. Numerous ghosts, especially from the *Mad Dog Killers* of previous years, are reported to roam the grounds.

A preservation society was formed which has capitalized on these spiritual happenings by offering ghost walks, tours, and Halloween happenings. Of course, sites used in the Shawshank film are also frequently visited by dozens of tourists each year including the Shawshank oak tree, nearby Malabar Farm, and the 1928 Renaissance Theatre now on the National Register of Historic Places which frequently shows the film. The thirteen spots from the surrounding area are on maps and websites as the faithful trekkers appear at all times of the year to relive their film experience by savoring the *real thing*.

The Shawshank phenomenon is also noteworthy since an actor, James Kisicki from Chester Township east of Cleveland, plays the part of a bank manager in the film. Kisicki relates that the original story, which was written by horror novelist and best-selling author Stephen King, was just an account of a friendship in prison but, because of massive interest after the movie became available on tape, turned into something much more.

Kisicki's scenes were shot inside of the bank building in Ashland; in honor of the 20th anniversary of the release of the film; he signed autographs for fans of the movie and discussed his role. He found it difficult to believe the publicity that *The Shawshank Redemption* continues to generate years after its release; although nominated for seven Academy Awards, the film didn't win a thing! Regardless, the endeavors fans will go through to get a "piece" of their favorite movie are unbelievable. One admirer even wanted to purchase Kisicki's clothes from his scenes!

Locals have also benefitted from the success and notoriety of the film. Souvenirs available from area stores include *Shawshank T-shirts*, *prison chocolate bars* from a local confectionery titled *The Squirrels Den, Prison Break Sodas* courtesy of *Richland Carrousel* and *Jailhouse Java Coffee* sipped at the unique *Blueberry Patch.*

Celebrations in previous years have garnered as many as 6,000 fans, eager to learn more about the stars, the film and the location sites, notably Mansfield Reformatory. The Visitors Bureau in Mansfield has bowed to the demand and created a website plus map to direct avid admirers from one location in the area to another.

It seems that *The Shawshank Redemption* and subsequently the *Mansfield Reformatory* will never die. The reformatory has successfully remade itself from a training camp in the Civil War to a prison to a tourist site complete with ghosts and goblins celebrating Halloween night. Who knows what will come next? Only the future will tell.

Author Bio:

Please see Linda Lehmann Masek's Bio elsewhere in this Anthology.

Lillian McNab and the Gerbil of Doom
by
Gerry Wolfson-Grande

Lillian McNab stepped into the large, walk-in closet and wrestled down the box of Halloween decorations. She was late getting them out this year; it was already October 3 and no wailing witches or moaning ghosts hung on her trees, no gleeful goblins peeked around the pilings of her picket fence. No wolves howled from the shadowy corners of the yard. And no mummies, zombies or vampires congregated around her front door. Maybe most people waited a little longer, but since Lillian lived in a house which could have hosted a horror movie, she felt it was appropriate to pay prompt and proper homage to the holiday.

She hauled the box out to the front parlor and began to extract its contents. Soon a dark heap of fearsome beasties and beings littered the sofa, chairs, coffee table, and even the floor. The average prosaic person might have wondered how they all fit in one box that one average-sized, middle-aged woman could handle. Such a person obviously would not have the mental capacity to consider the possibility that time and space are only as finite as the average perception considers them to be. Lillian had never been troubled by such details.

She picked up the wolf-shapes, flattened bodies flapping ludicrously in her hands, and trotted outside, distributing them in their respective corners. Each one received a pat on the head and a few muttered words in a language rarely heard in this day and age. The witches and ghosts followed. Passersby might smile tolerantly, positive they could see the cords suspending these phantasms, not realizing that the strings were the illusion.

Lillian returned to the parlor and snapped her fingers at the pile of goblins, which seemed to have rearranged itself while she was outside.

"All right, you lot. No fighting in the house. Outside with you, and don't dawdle. There's still plenty to wake, and I don't have the time to spend on your games."

The heap of brownish cloth leapt up, whirled around for a few minutes, and finally settled into several twinkling shapes consisting mostly of tatters and long, shining, very sharp teeth. They scuttled away, shrill shrieks and cackles drifting in their wake, as they ran to play hide and seek among the fence posts. Lillian sent a sniff of disapproval after them, which dissipated disconsolately when it was universally ignored.

Shaking her head, she returned to her task. Hauling all of the various odd shapes out of the box had tired her. With a few more guttural words, she settled for waving at them and pointing at the door as the contingent of vampires, mummies and zombies arranged itself before her.

She should have raised them first. The mummies gave her aggrieved looks of displeasure as they staggered around the hall, trying to loosen stiffened limbs, and a couple of the zombies needed a good brushing with a lint remover. What was left of their faces conveyed similarly censorious expressions. Annoyed, Lillian turned her attention to the vampires, almost daring them to express any criticism, but there were no takers. She shooed them all out impatiently, and returned to the parlor to check the box. Everything was outside, including a suitably scary Pumpkinhead and several unadorned companion pumpkins, courtesy of a neighboring farmer.

There was a knock and a thump at the door, and Lillian wondered if he had brought her more. She opened it and stared. On her doorstep sat a large object covered by a cloth, which she cautiously twitched off to find a wire-mesh cage. Inside crouched a hairy pudding with a tail. The cage bore a sign:

THE GERBIL OF DOOM.

"Just what am I supposed to do with this?" she wondered aloud.

From the innards of the cage, a deep, raspy voice replied, "You're the Halloween expert. Just wing it, lady."

Lillian bridled at the creature's rudeness, and started to move her fingers to transform it into something unpleasant, except what could be more obnoxious than a gerbil? While she dithered, a voice hailed her from next door, where she could see several flattish objects strewn about the yard.

"Great decorations this year, Miz McNab!"

Lillian shuddered as she saw the tall, gangly figure of her taste-challenged next-door neighbor Albert shambling towards her. The first Halloween after his arrival, a goofily grinning ghost and a dyspeptic looking witch, both inflatable, had adorned Albert's front lawn. With

Lillian's permission (encouragement even), her goblins had gleefully attacked the repulsive objects, only to find that there was in fact one thing goblins couldn't—or at least shouldn't—eat. After spewing soggy bits of plasticky goo over most of the yards along the street, the goblins had petulantly refused to go near Albert's yard again. Unfazed by the fate dealt his first decorations and the continuing disapproval of the local homeowners' association, Albert simply bought more and more, all disconcertingly immune to even Lillian's strongest spells.

Albert strolled up to her porch and squinted at the cage. "Whatcha got there, Miz McNab?"

"Oh, a friend sent it to me," Lillian said lightly, hoping her seeming lack of interest would convince him to go away.

No such luck. He was reading the sign, his lips moving then read it aloud. "The Gerbil of Doom, eh? Ha, ha. That critter looks as scary as my nephew's bunny rabbit."

Lillian heard an odd noise coming from the cage and looked down. The gerbil was grinding its tiny teeth. She felt a sudden tickle of camaraderie, and she smiled down at the ugly little beast.

"Well, Albert, you never know. One man's terror, and all that."

Albert gave her a blank look, then held up a small device.

"Got a whole bunch of new dee-cors for the yard this year. And they're all set up to inflate just with this little remote." He pressed some of the buttons, and Lillian watched with horror as an entire yardful of happy spooks and grinning cats, toothy pumpkins and – was that a Frankenstein's monster solemnly dancing to tinny harpsichord music emanating from its chest? She closed her eyes for a minute, hoping it was all a hallucination.

Albert mistook her expression for pleasure.

"I knew you'd like it!" he crowed. He waved at her while she was still speechless, and wandered back to his own domain, where he began to dance along with the monster.

"Oh, dear," Lillian breathed, once she could force out the words. "Now what are we going to do?" The gerbil cleared its throat, and she glanced down at it.

"What?"

"I don't suppose you've got any cigars," it said. She shook her head, and it sighed. "One could only hope. Not to worry, lady. They don't call me the Gerbil of Doom for nothing."

"Oh, yeah?" Lillian snapped. "And just what do Gerbils of Doom do, anyway?"

"Gerbil. Singular. I'm the one and only." Its face looked as smug as a fat rodentite face could, as it beckoned her closer and whispered in her ear.

"Are you sure this will work?" she asked, making little attempt not to sound dubious.

It yawned.

"Lady, you're the witch. I'm just the Gerbil of Doom."

Whatever that meant.

"All right, gerbil. Whatever it is you're going to do had better be effective, or the next spell is going to make you something far less potentially ominous."

She opened the cage, recited, "Burble, Ferble, Gerbil" with a moderately straight face and serious tone, and stood back.

The Gerbil of Doom yawned again, scratched its nose and butt with a claw tip, and then sauntered out of its cage with a wink and a nonchalant swagger.

"Next time don't forget the cigars, okay, lady?"

It strolled towards Albert's yard, growing as it went, until it easily dwarfed the decorations. One stomp obliterated the entire lot. Then the gerbil rang Albert's doorbell.

"Trick or treat."

"What the – "Albert began, his voice choking off abruptly as he was scooped up in a giant gerbil paw. His house met the same fate as the decorations, and the Gerbil of Doom turned and winked again at Lillian, who moved her fingers gleefully. A corn field appeared where Albert's lawn had been, harvest-ready stalks stretching upwards. The gerbil released its grasp, and the last part of the spell wrapped itself around Albert as the gerbil returned to Lillian's porch, shrinking as it bumped along.

Returned to normal size, the Gerbil of Doom hopped onto Lillian's lap and fixed her with a calm stare before flipping onto its back for a tummy scratch. Lillian gestured at the Pumpkinhead, and a yellow gleam emanated from its eyes and jagged grin. Lillian's monsters and beasties pursued their various interests in the yard as the goblins played hide and seek around the fence posts. And next door, two crows commented rudely on the tall, gangly appearance of the brand new scarecrow, which could only flap its hands ineffectually in response.

Retired (well, mostly) witch and Gerbil of Doom gazed contentedly at the scene before them. Tomorrow she was going to go buy it a whole carton of stogies. This was going to be a wonderful Halloween.

Author Bio:

Gerry Wolfson-Grande is a writer, editor, paralegal, and musician. She grew up in the Washington, D.C., area, with the exception of five years in Germany, and eventually set down roots in Orlando, Florida. She has a B.A. in history and a Master's in Liberal Studies from Rollins College in Winter Park, Florida. Her first published short story was "Not a Good Night at Ford's," published first in *Pulse Magazine* and then in *Under the Cosmic Sofa* (Partners in Crime, 2009), and which won a Florida Writers Association Royal Palm Literary Award. She has also published "Like," in *Pets Across America, Volume 3* (2011); "My Wheels Have Names," in *Wheels* (Florida Writers Association anthology 2012); and "The Chess Players," in *Slices of Life* (Florida Writers Association anthology 2010). "The Chess Players" is the first story in her novel-in-stories, *The Chess Players*, which she wrote as part of her graduate work and is currently revising in order to submit it for commercial publication. Her Halloween short story, "Lillian McNab and the Gerbil of Doom," was written partly as the result of a dare by a friend who, like Gerry, couldn't resist the idea of a story with a Gerbil of Doom in it.

A History of the Mysterious Halloween Maze

by
Linda Lehmann Masek

My great-uncle owned a farm in Bluffton, Ohio, sixty years ago. As a child I remember traveling past cornstalk covered fields in the late fall, playing with my cousins in these same fields, or just plain getting lost in the high cornstalks and wandering around for hours. On Halloween night my cousins and I, dressed in our costumes, would jump on and off the paths, scaring ourselves silly on the night when spooks and goblins roamed about. Little did I know that I was playing in something that had a long, intricate history, dating back thousands of years!

They were called labyrinths in ancient times, hedges in the later years and mazes in the United States. These convoluted *mystery paths* with their tunnels of trees, hedges or cornstalks become a delight for children and adults in the month of October throughout Ohio. Symbolizing harvest time in the United States and especially Ohio, these tunnels made of cornstalks have had a long and extremely interesting history.

The earliest mazes were those found in Egypt; the historian Herodotus in his writings described the underground labyrinths which led to the tombs of the Egyptian kings in the 5th century B.C. The early Greeks also had their labyrinths, discussed in Greek mythology. The most famous of these were the underground passages on the island of Crete in the city of Knossos. Legend states that a monster called the Minotaur lived inside this labyrinth, devoured human sacrifices and was finally slain by a Greek youth named Theseus who unraveled the secret of the passages to defeat the Minotaur in battle.

Labyrinths also had a religious significance; those in France were traversed by Pilgrims on a spiritual journey of faith. Constructed in black-and-white tiles, the most famous of these was at Chartres Cathedral. Scandinavian legends depict their labyrinths in stone on the coastline of the country, these were supposed to trap the violent winds that tortured the shores.

The most famous of the early mazes were the turf mazes in England. The playwright Shakespeare talked of mazes in his plays; the English labyrinths were regarded more as games with many paths inside, circling around and leading one in the wrong direction. Girls stood in the center while the boys of the village raced to see who could reach them first. A similar pattern was used with the hedge mazes which were combined with gardens of secret passages and flowers. Kent's Leeds Castle had the most famous of these mazes along with Hampton Court Palace, while Hever Castle added water to the maze to help confuse the issue even more!

The Victorian Age (1830-1910) was noted for the continued development of the mazes throughout the country. Formal gardens at the homes of the wealthy were a trend that symbolized the Victorian love of gardening and creative landscaping. More modern mazes included a mirror maze at the Wookey Hole Caves in Somerset complete with music and dancing fountain jets, while the Jersey Water Maze in the Channel Islands had over 200 water jets redesigning this unusual creation every minute.

The British love of gardening was exported to the country of South Africa along with the Soekershof Maze. This "walkabout" was characterized by the lush gardens found throughout the country melded with the hedge mazes common in England. Composed of hibiscus flowers and cactus, the Klaas Voogds Maze blossomed all year round; the maze depicted stories based on the folklore legends of the country. The mild climate of South Africa plus a huge variety of plants provided excellent conditions for the creation of beautiful mazes which could be spotted throughout the country.

The European mazes were the forerunners of those developed in the United States by the immigrants from the European lands. In 1935, a famous hedge maze was created at Colonial Williamsburg in Virginia while a brick pavement maze was on display in West Palm Beach, Florida.

The most well known American maze was the corn maze which has become more and more popular throughout the decades, especially at Halloween time. The forerunner of this creation originated in the designs of the Native Americans, particularly the Pima and Hopi Indian tribes, with the Hopi pueblo in Arizona displaying six labyrinth design dating back to 1200 A.D. Maize or corn mazes were used for fun for farm children in days of yesteryear; today these elaborate creations are an additional source of income for farm families. Designs have included such well known historical events as the Liberty Bell in Philadelphia, George Washington crossing the Delaware in the American Revolutionary War and the Titanic sailing from Southampton, England in 1912.

One of the most famous architects of the corn maze is Adrian Fisher whose creative maze work has been noted nationwide. Fisher is the world's most prolific maze architect; he has created over 500 mazes on six continents. His work has been displayed in "The Smithsonian Magazine", "National Geographic" and "People Magazine." Fisher's creations have graced the Wisconsin Dells, Skyline Caverns in Virginia and Wildwood, New Jersey. Three of his mazes have been credited in the *Guinness Book of World Records* as being the largest of their kind in Pennsylvania and Michigan.

Corn mazes are relatively simple to make; passages through the maze can be cut by hand or tractor and designs can be created individually or by a professional *maze designer*. The corn must be six feet tall, and passages need to be wide enough to accommodate families with children. Design can be relatively simple or complicated with the maze only lasting about two months until cold weather arrives.

Corn mazes can be found throughout the State of Ohio; Van Wert, Bowling Green, Fremont, Whitehouse, Findlay, Bluffton and Oregon are just some of the places that have turned to this popular game in the autumn. Adventure Acres in Bellbrook, Ohio near Dayton is credited with the largest corn maze of its kind in the United States!

Farmers have not only capitalized on the maze's popularity, they have added additional treats to the autumn months by sponsoring petting zoos with farm animals and pumpkin mazes and jamborees. These fun-filled cornstalk passages have come a long way since my rambles in Bluffton sixty years ago. Much more elaborate, mazes will only get bigger and better as *maze-fever* continues to sweep the country, and children and adults search for a rollicking good time in the autumn months leading up to Halloween. One fact seems to be indisputable – mazes are here to stay.

Author Bio"

Please see Linda Lehmann Masek's Bio on page 122 of this Anthology.

The Curdle Cat
by
Mark H. Newhouse

The Curdle Cat slinks through the moonlit streets. He is silent, black, yet almost invisible, like fog. His ember eyes follow every movement of the flickering lights in the houses that are placed like neat matchboxes along the sides of the suddenly ominous black asphalt. He searches hungrily for a soul, a child's soul.

It is Halloween.

The cat recognizes the house for which he has been searching. He remembers when he was a pet here, lying stretched in the child's arms, purring as her fingers played through his soft fur. The memory of what he has lost makes his eyes narrow. He raises his ghostly face toward the moon, letting out a chilling wail that pierces the darkness. It is this desolate cry that has given him his name. It is a painfully, mournful cry that curdles the blood.

The cat leaps to a limb on a skeletal tree. From this perch he sends his cold breath down on all who pass below. Costumed children gathering candy from neighborhood homes look up, stare into his hollow eyes, and shiver with fear.

He does not move. They are not his target.

In seconds the children forget and are off again in a mad rush to get more candy, before the night is too thick, and their mothers call them inside.

Suddenly the cat picks up the scent of the girl who held him when she was a child. He thinks her name was Laurie. His memory after death is clouded. He is surprised to see how much older she appears to be. Dressed in jeans and black vinyl jacket, she is walking with two boys, none of the three in costume. They say they are too old to wear costumes, too old for Halloween...too old to be frightened.

The boys break away from Laurie. They dash behind two trees down the street. A group of younger children are walking toward them, chattering happily through their masks.

Laurie hides nearby, knowing what is going to happen. Her heart speeds and her tongue runs across her glossed lips in anticipation.

The cat feels the adrenaline surging in Laurie's body as if it is his own. His eyes follow to where her eyes are aimed.

The young children, the age Laurie was just a few years ago, when she held the cat so tenderly, when she wanted the cat to sleep on her bed, are just passing under the twin trees.

The cat hears their sudden screams as Laurie's friends rush out from where they have been hiding, waving their arms and throwing eggs.

Laurie laughs as their terrified young prey drop their bags of candy and run to their homes, screams lingering.

Laurie's friends scoop up the bags and return to her laughing and bragging about what each of them did. She pops a toffee into her mouth, almost choking because she is laughing so hard.

The cat has watched it all. He hears the boys bragging, showing off for Laurie. He hears her laughing with them. His hair bristles, but he must wait. It is not time yet.

Laurie and her cohorts approach a house on the dimly lit street.

The taller boy, whispers to Laurie. He runs up to the porch, grabs a carved pumpkin and smashes it into juicy pulp in the middle of the road. The boy's rage, as he pounds the pumpkin's smiling face with his shoes, fuels the cat's fury.

The cat's stomach churns as Laurie slides her hand into this vandal's fist.

The shorter boy walks ahead, hiding a grimace as he observes their clutched hands. His tongue runs across his chapped lips which repeat Laurie's name whenever she can't hear. In the darkness of his bedroom, his eyes reach out to her window each night.

Laurie knows the other boy is watching so she reaches up and kisses the vandal holding her hand, letting him taste her toffee breath. She pulls away when he tries for more. "Later," she whispers, smiling slyly as the shorter boy walks quickly, to get even further away so he doesn't have to hear them.

The cat feels all these things, and wonders how the child he knew could have changed so much. He recognizes the icy cruelty inside her, the anger.

It is almost midnight. The smaller children are safely asleep. The cat hears the contented sounds of house cats as they crawl into bed. It torments him to know Laurie grew tired of him, no longer loved him. He hates her for letting him loose to become what he is now, a forever homeless spirit lusting for revenge.

Laurie's friends are prowling again. This time their target is a car. They swoop along its sleek sides with cans of shaving cream. They think it's only a little fun, a Halloween trick-or-treat.

The car alarm screeches. Lights and windows open in the nearby house.

The boys escape, tossing the spent shaving cream cans into the gutter as they race down the street, Laurie forgotten for the moment.

The cat tenses, but it isn't time yet.

Half a block away, the boys stop running, trying to catch their breath. They are laughing so hard they double over. "Did you see that old man running after us?"

Laurie rejoins them, scolding them for leaving her behind.

The vandal grins, grabs her hand and they are off again, roaming the streets, convinced they are the kings of Halloween.

A witch's silhouette crosses the moon. It is midnight.

The cat hears the distant clank of chains and the crunch of locks as the doors of the cemetery begin to open. The real Halloween has begun.

He moves toward Laurie.

It is the cat's curse to suffer the sensations Laurie feels, so he knows the girl, staring at the moon, has suddenly felt a fingernail of cold fear rush down her back.

"Did you feel that, Dan?" Laurie asks the tall boy.

"Feel what?" The boy holding her hand sneers.

The cat relishes the fear growing inside the girl. He glares at Dan and Laurie's clasped hands. He exhales suddenly into the boy's face, the smell of rotting flesh and dry blood.

"Don't do that," the boy shouts, throwing down Laurie's hand.

"What," Laurie asks, "I didn't do anything!"

The boy rubs his face with his free hand, the other clutching his stolen bag of candy. "You breathed on me! Get a mint!"

"Forgive me for living!" Laurie stomps away.

"I'm sorry," the boy says too low for her to hear. His eyes search in vain for the menacing creature that he suddenly senses is dangerously near.

The cat hurls his body at the boy's face, his paws cleaving the air and his throat releasing a blood-curdling cry.

The boy screams and drops his candy bag to the ground.

Laurie turns just fast enough to see the boy running away, the echo of his terrified screams remaining long after he is out of sight.

The cat feels Laurie's fear harden like a knot around her throat. She tries to call the second boy, but no sounds escape. The cat remembers how the poison gas filling his lungs, when nobody came to claim him, silenced his cries for her in the last seconds of his existence.

The second boy is appraising Laurie, suddenly standing in the middle of the street all alone. He smells opportunity. He hurries toward her, eyes full of hope. He looks past her, on all sides, to see if his friend is lurking near, ready to spring at him if he makes a move. He wants to take her hand in his own sweaty paw, but knows he must be cautious. As he approaches, he doesn't see the fear that is growing in Laurie's eyes.

Suddenly the boy stops walking. His nose has picked up a strange, pungent scent, the cat's scent, the smell of the dirt of the graveyard, bone and flesh, a musty thickness that envelops his skin like an ever-tightening shroud, clogging his nostrils and burning his eyes. He coughs, a painful fit of coughing, but he doesn't leave. This is his chance at Laurie, now that Dan is gone. He won't be driven away!

He moves toward Laurie again, fighting the acrid smell, stifling the hacking cough. His eyes are on Laurie. She looks so vulnerable.

The cat rubs his petrified fur along the boy's legs. Even the thick armor of jeans does not protect from the harsh scraping of wire hairs against the boy's hairless flesh.

The boy reaches down, raises his pant leg, tries to scratch away the invisible thing that is scraping his flesh like steel wool. He stares in puzzlement. There is nothing there.

The cat only wants the girl. The boys are nothing to him, insignificant impediments, nameless souls for some other ghost to harvest. But this boy is stubborn. He refuses to leave.

The cat steals forward and punctures the boy's shin with a sharp nail that can penetrate metal.

The boy stares down at his uncovered leg, dismayed to see a thin trickle of blood. "I'm not leaving," he shouts to the unhearing night, to the demon that is torturing him. "I'm not leaving!"

His cries frighten Laurie more than any other sound she has ever heard because she does not see his attacker…only the boy, terrified eyes darting in all directions, hands struggling to hold up his pants legs while fighting off the invisible demons.

The cat strikes again and then again, just deep enough to leave tiny, unstoppable, trails of blood on those pale, hairless legs.

The boy backs away, his eyes still locked on Lorie, but now in fear. A fever is rising in him, and he hears his own heart pounding. He searches wildly around for his invisible tormentor, flailing his arms to protect his flesh.

The cat, losing patience, lets out a shrill wail.

The sound of all that pent-up loneliness and pain fills the boy with excruciating fear.

The sound stretches endlessly and echoes hollow tin as the second boy finally giving up on his hopes for Laurie, runs away. The candy bag, long forgotten, is lying on the asphalt road, as he scrambles toward the house he hates, but will now hide in every Halloween.

The cat turns his attention at last toward Laurie. The girl is in his eyes.

He makes himself a shadow, allowing her to see his slinking shape.

Laurie is unable to move under the spell of the cat's empty eyes.

The cat is consumed by his need to get even, to pay back those who had abandoned him when he was no longer a cute kitten. His mouth waters, blood red saliva dripping from his lips. He is close to taking the girl's soul.

The ghost soaks in Laurie's terror. He smells the odors of fear, the terror of knowing she can't escape whatever it is that is hunting her, the invisible Halloween creatures that have frightened the others away. He savors this panic welling up inside her. He wants to taste each moment of it...to make the torment last until the last second before dawn when he will snatch her soul and drag her to be with him forever.

On Halloween, the ghost cat is allowed to reshape into the being he was before they led him away with the thick rope into the gas chamber, the last room of his life.

He moves toward Laurie, his eaten away corpse concealed now by flesh and black fur.

He rubs his restored body against her ankles as he did when he was hers.

She looks down startled.

"Where did you come from?"

He circles her ankles again. He has time to play this game of cat and mouse.

Laurie reaches toward him.

He arches away, snarls, his teeth and claws threatening to tear into her.

"Now! Do it now!" screams his brain.

She pulls away her hand.

Cat and mouse – he approaches again, concealing his knife-sharp claws.

"Nice cat," she suddenly says. "I won't hurt you."

He stops moving. Her voice is timid, child-like again.

"You're a nice cat," she says in a soothing tone.

He backs away, his fangs hidden by twisted, ash-colored lips.

"You don't have to be afraid of me," the girl says. "I won't hurt you."

He is surprised to feel her hand drop down on his back with the lightness of a breeze. His breathing stops.

Laurie's hand ruffles his fur as it slowly moves up and down his back.

"Doesn't that feel nice?" she asks. "I'll bet you're afraid too." She lets out a little sigh. "I was really scared," she says, "until you came along."

The cat, feeling the once familiar sensation of her fingers soothing him, slowly taking control of him, stretches out under her hand against his will, his body begging for more.

He wants revenge, to hurt her as he has been hurt, but something inside him is being reawakened by the unexpected gentleness of her touch. the satin texture of her voice.

"I once had a kitten," she says, "He was beautiful. I loved him a lot."

The cat tries to pull away. He doesn't want to hear this! It's too late!

"Don't worry," the girl holds him. "I'm not going to hurt you."

The cat can afford to be patient. He lets her continue.

"I called him Pepper, because he was black...like you," the girl says, still rubbing his fur. "It was a long time ago."

I hated that name, the cat thinks, but he really didn't.

"I used to love that kitten, especially when I'd sneak him into my bed," Laurie smiles at the memory. "I'll bet you've never slept in a bed your whole life, you poor thing," she says. "I wish I could take you home with me."

The cat tenses. The liar, he thinks, fury building inside. She is so frightened she'll say anything!

"I still miss my Pepper...." The girl frowns. "I was so angry when my parents told me we couldn't keep him. I hated them!" A tear rolls down the girl's face. It smudges her make up. It falls on the cat and sizzles like a burning coal. "I still do! I hate them. I hate them."

The cat peering deep into Laurie's soul, knows she is telling the truth. He realizes now Laurie had never wanted to abandon him. In plumbing her soul, he sees she has been abandoned too.

The ghostly cat is surprised to feel the hate that had been knotting inside him for so long, begin to cool. He had wondered how someone could love a pet, a kitten or puppy, and then abandon them when they were grown. He had hated her for that! He had hated her for thrusting him into a life of starvation, a life of hiding from predators that lurk in dirty alleys and gutters…terrifying, heartless creatures such as he had become. He had cursed her for that, and for the last days in the animal shelter, for the last agonized breaths of his fading body as he had sucked in the gas in that hollow room that echoed the last beats of his screaming heart.

He had come back to lure her to the end of Halloween, to torment her with fear, to keep her soul with him and the other damned spirits forever, but he now knows the girl is already fatally wounded. She is not the same Laurie that had held him so lovingly in her arms, had laughed and sung in the once warm and happy house.

He feels the endless depth of her pain. He knows that like he was before her, she has been abandoned, left to survive on her own. Her soul screams of parents too busy warring with each other to feel Laurie's anguish, to hear her cries.

Halloween is nearly over.

Laurie sits in the gutter, another stray.

Pepper lets Laurie hold him, stroke him. He feels his corporeal body slipping away. He trembles, tries to resist, struggles desperately to hold onto life, to hold onto Laurie.

He unleashes a final, terrifying, keening wail of heartbreaking pain, his paws turning to smoke, unable to hold her, unable to help her. He slips away, knowing he is already forgotten, tormented that Laurie must remain behind, wandering alone in the streets, raising her hollow eyes to the unanswering sky, and letting out a chilling, mournful cry… like a Curdle Cat.

Author Bio:

Mark H. Newhouse, author of Curdle Cat, which was earlier published in Cats by Fireside Publications, was born in Germany to Holocaust survivors, Mark loved teaching in Central Islip, New York, and SUNY Old Westbury, and was Elementary/Secondary Teacher of the Year (New York State Reading Assoc., 1989). To help combat bullying, he created The Bullystoppers Handbook, and other materials, free at www.bullystoppersclub.com.

Mark's books include: the 5 Star rated, *ECTOS: The Ghost Doctor's Assistant; Ectos 2: The Burning* (Solstice Publishing); *The Rockhound Science Mysteries,* winner of Learning Magazine's Teachers' Choice Award; and *The Midnight Diet Club,* a humorous novel about bullying, First Prize, YA fiction, Florida Writers Association, now also an audiobook (Audible.com.) He also authored, *How to Sell Your Books Checklist* (AimHi Press), and his stories have been winners in the Writers' Digest, Creative Writer's Notebook, (Journeys anthologies), and other competitions.

Mark co-produced and hosted, *Author's Beat,* available free at www.authorsbeat.com. A member of the *Author's Guild, SCBWI and Florida Writer's Association,* he co-founded, was first president of the *Writer's League,* and is *Top* Cat of the *Children's Authors Team,* where he was chief editor of *Holiday Helpings* and *The Story Shop* anthologies. Receiving his BA and MA from Queens College, New York, he now resides in Florida, where he enjoys visiting schools and libraries to inspire children to read and write.

The Last of the Soul Mates
by
By Jessica Henderson

Flying through the trails on the out skirts of the McCane property, Nic caught a glimpse of a fine-looking lass sitting on a log across the creek. She didn't belong there, he was sure, because he knew everyone in town; and he had never seen her before. The McCane's were an odd bunch, and they certainly didn't have any beautiful girls with long flowing hair in their family.

He wanted to help her – she looked so cold and lost, just staring at the nearly empty pumpkin patch in the distance, bordered by an eerie-looking cornfield farther on – but the creek was too wide and deep for him to get his snow mobile across at that point. Everything on her side of the creek looked plucked and ready for the Halloween ghosts and goblins that would soon be out in force.

Nic knew a way if he could still find it; he would have to go about a half-mile down the road to the narrow spot in the creek where someone had built a plank bridge across the water; it would be strong enough for him and his vehicle. There was even a spot where he could hide his cruiser so no one would see it and know that he had trespassed on their property. He got to where the girl was sitting in no time after hiding his snow cruiser under some brush.

"Hi, there, I'm Nic," he said, by way of introduction. "Y' look kinda lonely out here by yourself. Anything I can do to help?"

"This town is very strange." She said. "People around here have scary eyes and don't like to talk very much."

Nicholas chuckled while taking off his camo hoodie.

"You're freezing. You'll get sick if we can't warm you up." He wrapped the hoodie around the girl.

"Follow me; you shouldn't be out here." He grabbed her hand then stopped suddenly when she wouldn't move.

"Where are we going?"[i] It doesn't look like you're going back the same way I came from." She began to shiver and stutter. "I...I just moved here about a week ago and my aunt told me not to go far; she told me not to…"

Nic saw a flicker out of the corner of his eye while she was talking and knew by the jagged movements and flashes of color that it was time to go. He yanked her up off the log.

"Let's go!" he yelled and began running. Nicholas' grip was so tight that she had no choice but to follow.

The girl tried to slow him down; she wanted to ask him what on Earth was going on, but Nicholas was running so fast it took all her strength to keep from falling down and stopping completely.

He didn't speak as they slowed down almost to a crawl. They could see a cabin a short distance ahead, dimly lit by a fire flickering in the fireplace. Dusk was approaching, and they heard the faint sound of wolves in the distance, howling and barking at some unknown prey.

"By the way, my name is Nicholas. Sorry for not introducing myself back there. I'm sure there are a great many things you still don't know about this place."

She smiled at him.

"Like…?"

Nic just looked at her. He appeared a bit confused and unfocused, becoming aware that she knew what he was talking about.

"Why don't we go knock on the door? Maybe they have a phone so I can call my aunt, or maybe…"

Nic interrupted.

"Wait! Shh! You see those people? Over there by the barn?"

He pointed to a large opening in the woods on the other side of the property, camouflaged by a ton of brush and snow.

"There's no barn." she said, "nothing there at all, just woods."

As she spoke, the people veered in their direction then quickly turned back, walking into a dark entrance to a pathway leading into the woods.

"There, that's it – the doorway into the barn. D'you see it?"

Pointing in that direction, Nic excitedly traced his fingers around what he thought to be the barn.

"Oh… yes, I *do* see it," she said. "I can't believe it; how is that even possible?" She stared ahead, unable to take her eyes off it.

"I don't know, but there are a lot of things around here that I can't explain and that don't seem real. We need to get to my snow mobile; it's parked a little ways passed the barn. I have it hidden under some brush so no one would know I'm out here – speaking of which, how did you manage to get all the way out here without being seen? This is *supposed* to be private property."

"Let's go!" Without waiting for an answer, he grabbed her hand, and they both began to run towards his snow mobile.

"Where are we going Nicholas?" she gasped.

"Outta here!" he said as they made it to his snow mobile, hopped on and took off. Nic sped through the trails and up and down the hills. He didn't stop for anything. It was only a couple of miles back to the main road to town. After that, it only took them a minute on the cruiser to get to the first light in town.

"Where do you live?" he asked her.

"In the cottage around the corner from the baker."

Nic knew exactly where the girl lived because he delivered the Daily Talk, the town's daily newspaper. Hers was the house added to his route last Monday.

"Hey I deliver your news paper," he giggled. "I was just here this morning. What a coincidence. Just before the sun came up, I thought, *I wonder who finally moved into this old place?*"

As she climbed off the snow cruiser, she said, "Now you know, and thank you for helping me out of woods. I could have been in real trouble if you hadn't shown up." She smiled up at Nic. "By the way, my name is Whisper – just in case you're interested."

"I'm interested," he said, laughing at himself. "Sorry, I should have asked you sooner."

Nicholas reached out his hand,

"Hi, Whisper," he said, "Pleased to meet you."

No lights were on inside the cottage. Seven o'clock; the street lights were on, and all was quiet in the small town.

"Not much goes on around here, huh?"

"Not really, I mean, nothing fun and exciting, if that's what you mean." Nic started up his snow mobile and put it into gear. "You should go inside and get warmed up; get some rest. The cold here is a lot different from other places, once you've been in it for too long it seems as if you can never get warm. I'll stop by tomorrow if it's okay, and show you around."

He grinned.

"Only so you don't get lost again. We can take a look at all the Halloween decorations, too. All Hallows Eve will be coming up soon – maybe a party or two…?"

Whisper rolled her eyes.

"Thanks again. Yes. Yes. I think it will be okay if you come by. I definitely don't want to get lost again. I had no idea how to get out of there until you came along. I just got lost in how appealing the fall evening looked as the sun was going down. Never should have gone out there unprepared. I didn't mean to stay so long; it kind of just happened. You know?"

She grabbed a spare key out from underneath the doormat and unlocked the front door.

"Yeah, I know. Time has a strange way of passing quickly when you're out there alone."

"Sure does.

"You shouldn't go too far until you know your way around better. See ya tomorrow."

"Okay, Nic. Thanks for rescuing me."

"Anytime." He nodded, with a slight smirk on his face. "Good night Whisper, it was nice to meet you."

Nic revved up his cruiser and pulled off.

He threw his fingers up in a peace sign as she waved good bye.

Nicholas lived with his Uncle Jack. He had no rules to follow; no curfew and his uncle, a mountain tour guide, was hardly ever home. Uncle Jack was gone a lot of the time on camping trips with people, teaching them how to survive in the cold and how to hunt, fish, and live off the land.

Thrill seekers, hikers, vacationers, campers – anybody and everybody – seemed to come to Uncle Jack to go up the mountain. His unique skills in all areas of survival, and his training in handling emergency situations, make him the *go-to guy* for the paramedics when they need help with a rescue mission. This has been happening more and more lately – so much so that Miss Lydia, their part time house lady had to move in last week. She used to only come every other day to make sure the laundry was done, and there was food for Nic to eat.

After meeting up with a couple of friends and hanging out at the corner Malt Shop, it was around nine p.m. when Nic finally walked through the doors of his family's five-bedroom home. The house, which had belonged to Nic's parents, is enormous compared to most of the other homes in Kindrick. Many of the other homes are cottages and very few even have an upstairs. None of the others have an attic the size of a small house like Nic's. His Uncle had inherited the place when Nic's parents went missing fifteen years ago.

Nicholas's parents were married at the highest peak on the mountain. Every year after, they took a trip up to that same spot for their anniversary. Nic was four-years-old when his parents disappeared from their mountaintop hideaway. Uncle Jack had always watched Nicolas, so it only seemed right that Jack keep him after they were gone. Although he would never admit it, Nic's Uncle takes solo trips up the mountain every so often. Nic and Lydia believe that he is still searching for any clues as to what might have happened to the couple.

"Uncle Jack has been gone for a lot longer this trip, hasn't he?" Nic said as he kicked his shoes off at the front door.

"Yes he has, hasn't he?" Miss Lydia said while grabbing a plate of food out of the microwave.

"I heard you pulling up, and I *know* you probably haven't fed yourself today... Have you? I'm starting to worry about you Nic," she said as she put the plate on the table.

"You have nothing to worry about Miss Lydia, I'm fine. Will it make you feel better if I stop in during the day and have some lunch?"

Nic had a mischievous grin on his face as he took a huge bite of the meatloaf she had made for him.

"What's going on with you? I haven't seen a grin like that on you... in ... well I've never seen you grin like that Nicholas!"

Lydia hurried over and sat across form Nic at the table. She squinted her eyes and smiled as she made a funny face at him like she was silently inviting him to tell her everything.

"So... who is she?" Nic choked on the potatoes and had to take a drink to clear his throat.

"Why do you think there is a girl? And so what if I'm grinning. Maybe I'm just hungry and I love your meatloaf."

He kept shoveling the food into his mouth as if he were never going to get to eat again. Lydia silently waited for him to finish and observed him. Every time Nic looked at her a little grin would appear on the side of his face. When he finished, she grabbed his plate up and washed it right away.

"Pie?" She cut a piece of pie for the each of them.

"So..." Lydia pushed the plate closer to Nic and handed him a fork. "Who is she?"

Nic took a bite of the pecan pie and began speaking while he was still chewing. "Whisper. She and her aunt just moved into that cottage around the corner from the baker. That's all you are getting because that is all I know." Nic gobbled up the rest of his pie and burped.

"I knew it!" Miss Lydia sat there pleased with herself as Nic excused himself from the table.

"I'm gonna go grab a shower and hit the sack," he started to run up the stairs two at a time. "Thanks for dinner and as always, the pie was great Miss Lydia. Good night."

"Good night Nicholas, I laid out all your clean clothes on your bed. Could you at least put them away?"

The bathroom door slammed.

Lydia sat at the table finishing her pie, sighing and smiling to herself. "It's about time." She said to herself while washing up the few dishes in the sink. "It's about time."

It was still dark when Nic woke up. It was staying dark longer and longer these days. Not because of the time of year or the changing of the seasons. Something was about to happen. He could feel it in his bones. Something was coming. He shook his head a little, back and forth.

Every day for the past couple of weeks when he woke up, he would get flashes in his head of his mother reaching out to him and calling for him to help. And, during the day, when he's out riding he could hear voices vaguely through the distance. It only happened when he got close to the mountain pass – like someone calling out to him, luring him in closer. That's why he had been out riding his snow cruiser so much. That's how he found Whisper.

Nothing happens by chance, he thought. *It's all for a reason;* and he couldn't figure it out.

After getting dressed and pulling his boots on, Nic grabbed the breakfast bag that Miss Lydia had packed for him and left out the night before. She knows if she doesn't make it for him, chances are he won't eat until he is starving. And she wasn't about to let that happen. He made his way through his morning paper route with ease and finished up at Whisper's house. Amazingly she was waiting for him on her front porch step.

"Ready?" Nic asked with a smile.

"Yep." She jumped up and ran over to his snow cruiser. "Geesh, it's so cold in the mornings! Burr!" Whisper laughed out loud as she hopped on and wrapped her arms around Nic.

"Hold on..." He said as he pulled on the throttle and sped off.

"Where would you like to go first my lady?" he said as they approached the towns end. "Kindrick isn't very big is it?" she asked.

"Big enough, for people like us I guess." He slowed the cruiser down to minimum speed, and they trotted along the creek side.

"How about there?" She pointed to the mountain pass just ahead.

"NO." he said firmly. "There is nothing up there but snow."

He started to turn the opposite direction, but Whisper pulled on his jacket. "You said anywhere I want...Right? I want to go up there. Now, please."

He dropped his head in a sulking manner, and turned the handle bars towards the mountain pass. The one he had been avoiding for quite some time now.

"Here we go. Hold on tight, I don't want you to fall off." As they made their way up the pass, the voices became clearer. He recognized the voice immediately, his mother.

"Nicholas! Nicholas! Wake up, please you've got to get up! Please!" He heard these words vaguely as he began to come to. Everything was spinning, and his head was pounding with pain.

"What... what happened?" He managed to get out the words before relaxing his head back into the snow.

"You yelled something and drove us right into the mountain side. Lucky for us it was not solid land; it's actually an opening to a cave or something. Please, you've got to get up! We can't stay out here, its freezing."

Whisper began to cry. The thought of being stuck outside in the cold with no way of getting back – she didn't know how to start a snow mobile let alone tinker with it to see what was wrong with it. Nic was falling in and out of consciousness and, she had to think fast.

She took her jacket off, and leaned him up against his cruiser, covering him up. *Now is not the time to be scared Whisper,* she told herself. She cleared away some brush and found her way into the tunnel. She discovered that after a couple of yards, there was an opening to what looked like an underground room.

Quickly, she hurried back to Nicholas and drug him into the cave room. After getting him settled, she put her jacket back on and headed back outside to find some wood to burn. Within ten minutes or so she had enough sticks to get a nice fire burning and had a reserve pile on standby.

Nic had a backpack on the back of his snowmobile full of bottled water, protein bars, flash lights and batteries. He also had a tool kit in there, but she was not mechanically inclined. The two would have to wait until Nic came to so he could tinker with his snow mobile and get it running. She said a little prayer before falling asleep from exhaustion.

It seemed like she only closed her eyes for a second. When she woke, Nicholas was sitting up by the fire looking at her.

"You're okay!" she said as she sat up.

"Yeah, I'm so sorry, Whisper. I hope you didn't get hurt. Thank you. You saved my life you know. I can't believe you were able to drag me all the way back here. I don't know how you did it... but thank you so much. What happened?"

He tossed some sticks into the fire. She scooted closer.

"You yelled something and then we crashed."

"So you think that just because she saved his life, he will fall in love with her? C'mon, things like that happen every day. That doesn't mean they will live happily ever after." said the dark and deep voice ascending up the hallway to the cathedral where the Angel Gabriel sat.

"No I don't. In fact I know that is not what is going to cause them to fall in love," Gabriel said in a condescending tone.

"I know you have already intervened, Gabriel. "The form of a man began to materialize sitting on a sofa. "Come, come now, if you believe that, then the world is already yours. Everything is lost and I wouldn't still be standing here."

Gabriel laughed out loud and pranced around in a subtle way as if celebrating an early victory over his rival.

"We shall see. We shall see," said the figure. "All of the soul mated pairs haven't succeeded in finding each other before the end of their mortal lives up until now.

"So what makes you think these two will figure out they were made for each other before one of them dies? That accident was supposed to kill them both.

"Their mother's connection with them is stronger than anticipated."

"They will prove to be a great aggravation to me."

"No matter! My centuries are close by at all times. They will find out where the mothers are slipping through our borders soon."

The war between the heavens and the underworld has been going on for millennia. Slowly, one by one, couple by couple, the underworld has taken away peoples trust, faith in others, and love for each other. If the one or both of the kindred spirits perish before they realize they were made for each other, all will be lost and the underworld will finally have won the war. For there will be no one left who has faith, trust, or love for another. Nicholas and Whisper need to fall in love to break the malevolent spell that has cursed both their families and the rest of the world. Darkness and despair will be all that is left if they cannot find it within themselves to love, trust and to have faith in each other.

"This is going to sound crazy but, right before I blacked out, I swear I heard my mother's voice. It was like she was calling out to me for help." Nic stood up to walk over and sit next to Whisper.

She scooted over a little to give him more room to sit beside her.

"No it doesn't." She kicked some pebbles towards the fire and took a deep breath.

"I have been hearing my mother's voice, too. It feels like she has been guiding me. That's why I moved here with my aunt. Everything I have been doing lately is because it feels like something is urging me to. I feel like we are both here for a reason."

Her eyes began to water as she spoke.

"Nicholas, I feel like we were brought together." She blinked and a single tear fell down her cheek.

Nic wiped it away with his thumb.

"I do too," he said. "When you are near me, I feel this over whelming urge to protect you. I couldn't stop thinking about you from the first moment I saw you. Please don't think I'm a weirdo for saying all this being that we just met. I just feel like I know you, like... like I want to be around you. I've lost complete faith in people. No one seems to care about anything anymore. I see that everywhere I go. But you bring lightness with you and a calmness that is contagious."

Whisper began to blush, and a half smile revealed a cute little dimple so unnoticeable it almost wasn't there.

"You're just saying that."

"That was pretty suave though if I do say so myself, lover boy."

She started to scoot over as she became over-whelmed with flashbacks of all the other times guys had hit on her with only the intentions of taking her home. She'd never really had a boyfriend, or a great reason not to trust what Nic had just said. A few bad experiences were enough to ruin it for any guy who ever tried to be genuine to her in the future. She paused in her movement.

"Oddly enough though, I do have very similar feelings when you are around. That has to mean something. I'm sorry for my initial reaction to what you said a minute ago. I don't trust people either. And boy have I lost my faith in guys as well."

Nic scooted closer.

"I truly meant what I said, Whisper. I have never had these feelings in my head, or react to a person the way I do to you. I most certainly have never met a girl that could carry a guy into a cave during a snow storm and build a fire to keep them from freezing. You're very crafty and brave. You should be proud of yourself. I should have been the one saving you."

She let out a little laugh.

"You already did, remember?"

Nic's eyes widened.

"Yes, but..." Before he could finish, Whisper stood up and grabbed his bag. "You think you feel up to looking at your snow mobile? Maybe it's something simple, and we can get back to civilization." She handed him his cross-over and stood there looking at him as if she had just issued her first order in command.

"What's the rush? You don't have to fear me. I'm not going to do anything you don't want me to do," he said with a cheesy grin on his face.

"Ugh! You are being silly now. I know you won't do anything. I was just thinking that maybe you needed to get to a doctor, so you can get your head checked out."

He rubbed his head and squinted a little then shrugged his shoulders in a mocking way to show her he was fine.

"See? I'm fine, nothing to worry about. Besides, it's late and my headlight is broken on my cruiser. Even though I know this place like the back of my hand, I haven't been up this pass in a long time. I don't want to risk us getting lost and stuck out in the below freezing temperatures with nothing to shield us from the weather. Odds are we will be safer here for the night. If that's okay with you my lady." He bowed his head and held his hand out like a pawn seeking approval from his queen.

Whisper laughed out loud and shook her head in agreement.

Throughout the rest of the night, the two talked and laughed like old friends catching up on all the time that had passed in each other's absence. The fire was blazing, and the two were comfortably warm and cozy. When they grew sleepy, Whisper snuggled up right next to Nicholas.

He had a blow-up pillow in his pack, along with a blanket. Before falling asleep, Nic held her close. His heart swelled with a feeling of love for her as he turned his head to look into her eyes. She turned toward him, and their lips met. They melted into each other's arms and lay, holding each other through the night. The two woke still holding each other. Neither could explain it, but both knew in their hearts that they were inexplicably in love with one another. The last of the living soul mates had found one another and unknowingly won the war between the Heaven's and the Underworld.

"Until next time Gabriel," the black form faded as it descended down the cathedral hallway.

"And you shall lose again and again, my friend," Gabriel sat back and threw his feet up with a sigh of relief.

"Good-bye old friend."

Author Bio:

Jessica Henderson is a stay-at-home mom to four youngsters ranging in age from five-years to twelve-years old. She uses her creative talents to teach them a love of growing plants and the outdoor world along with indoor crafts during inclement weather. She had some help writing this story; Julia and Jake, 12 and 9 respectively, dictated some of the scenes and dialogue while 7-year-old Kadin cleared Nana's pantry of all the donuts and cookies, and 5-year-old Kira did what little sisters are supposed to do – pestered her siblings. *The Last of the Soul Mates*, a YA story, is Jessica's first official submission of her writing for publication.
Well done, Jessica.

Other Select Books Published by Fireside Publications

The Crystal Angel: by Olivia Claire High
Rose Cottage: by Olivia Claire High
Dreams: Shadows of the Night: by Olivia Claire High
Essays: On Living with Alzheimer's Disease:
  The First Twelve Months: by Lois Wilmoth-Bennett
The Furax Connection: by Stephen L. Kanne
The Find: by James J. Valko
Above Honor: Rachel's Story: by Donald Himelstein
Beyond Forever: by Taylor Shaye
The Cleansing: by B.F. Eller
The Long Night Moon: by Elizabeth Towles
The Cost of Justice: by Mike Gedgoudas
18 Days in September: by Allen N.Hunt, Ph.D
Independence Day Plague:by Carla Lee Suson
Odds & Ends ~Bits & Pieces: by Joye O'Keefe
The Serpent Sea: by Linda Lehmann Masek
Where Danger Lurks: by J udith Groudine Finkel
Texas Justice: by Judith Groudine Finkel
Ice Rose: by Alison Neuman
Raven April: by Nelson Trout
Searching for Normal: by Alison Neuman
The Wolf Deception: by Olivia Claire High

COMING SOON

Kari's Destiny~ No More Tomorrows: by Olivia Claire High

Published by: Fireside Publications

www.ingramcontent.com/pod-product-compliance
Lightning Source LLC
Chambersburg PA
CBHW070828180626
46818CB00001B/435